DEMCO

Act I, Act II, Act Normal

Martha Weston

Act I, Act II, Act Normal

Roaring Brook Press

Brookfield, Connecticut

Copyright © 2003 by Martha Weston
Published by Roaring Brook Press
A Division of The Millbrook Press
2 Old New Milford Road,
Brookfield, Connecticut 06804

Library of Congress Cataloging-in-Publication Data
Weston, Martha.
Act I, act II, act normal / Martha Weston.
p. cm.
Summary: Topher Blakely gets the lead in the eighth-grade play, but
unfortunately the play is "Rumpelstiltskin," the class bully picks on
him relentlessly, and his beloved cat dies, all of which teach him a lot
about compassion, friendship, and life.
[1. Theater—Fiction. 2. Schools—Fiction. 3. Family life—Fiction.]
I. Title: Act one, act two, act normal. II. Title: Act I, act II, act normal. III. Title.
PZ7.W52645 Ac 2003
[Fic]—dc21   2002014222

ISBN 0-7613-1779-1 (trade edition)
10 9 8 7 6 5 4 3 2 1
ISBN 0-7613-2859-9 (library binding)
10 9 8 7 6 5 4 3 2 1

Book design by Filomena Tuosto
Printed in the United States of America

First edition

THIS IS FOR CHARLEY,
THE actOR

Special thanks to Dave Mohler, D.V.M.,
for making sure the information about feline diabetes is correct.

And thanks to Rachel,
who asked the question in the first place.

Act I, Act II, Act Normal

THE SWEET TOOTH OF DEATH

"You are the murderer!" (Man, I love that line.)

Everyone screams. (Also a favorite moment.)

"The missing key, a dead parakeet for an alibi—it all leads right to you, Little Candy Apple!" Then I whip off her wig and sunglasses, and *ta da!* There is the face of an eighth-grade boy with a buzz cut.

Everyone screams again.

(*Curtain*)

My English class burst into applause. I, Christopher Blakely—Topher, to my friends—bowed deeply. Next to me, bowing and turning a little red, was the playwright himself, my best friend, Kip, who had read the part of Little Candy Apple.

"That was fantastic, Kip," said Mr. Griffin. "Of course,

I can't make predictions, but your script sounds like a winner to me."

Sure to Win

"I knew it! I knew it! I knew you would win!" We were on our way home, and I was this close to jumping up and down like some dork.

"But I *haven't* won," said Kip. "We don't find out until tomorrow, and there are four other finalists."

"Details," I said, brushing hair out of my eyes and readjusting my cap. "Did you see how everyone was totally surprised? Plus, they thought it was hilarious. And sick, too. You really put some gross stuff in there. That bit with the dead parakeet—did you see Brittani? I thought she was going to barf!"

"Yeah," agreed Kip, grinning. "That part worked better than I thought it would. And you were a riot as Detective Slade. If I do win, and I'm not saying I will, I know you'll get that part."

"Man, I hope so," I said. "I've wanted a lead since sixth grade. And I know all the lines."

"You should," said Kip. "This has always been *your* part—plus, you even helped me write some of it."

We reached the bus and hopped on, just as it was about to pull out.

"It's all timing," I said, as we got the last two seats together. "The timing this year is exactly right for the winner to be written by a guy, since it was a girl last year, and for them to pick a mystery, since it was a musical last year. It's perfect."

And the Winner Is . . .

After school the next day, everyone who was even thinking of trying out for the Hope Springs Middle School student play was in the school theater. We were all stoked to hear the announcement of the winning script. Even with hardly any Populars or Jocks—most would never be caught dead in a play—it was a pretty impressive crowd.

"Geez, auditions are going to be rough," I said. "I bet there'll be a lot of pissed-off kids when they don't get a part."

"Oh, great, that's all I need," muttered Kip.

Some middle-aged bald guy in baggy brown pants was waving his arms for people to hush. Gradually the room grew quiet. "All right! Excellent turnout. My name is Theodore Caparelli, and I'm the new director of plays here at Hope Springs. I'm looking forward to many exciting productions at this school."

People shuffled and squirmed in their seats, waiting for him to cut to the chase.

"Now, considering how many of you are here, I think you will be especially pleased about the winning script." Mr. Caparelli ran a hand over his shiny head, glancing down at a clipboard.

"In the past, the small cast size of many winning plays

has made it hard to include all the students who would like to participate. So this year, the review committee has chosen a winner not only with a superior and humorous script, but one that can accommodate a large cast."

"Uh-oh," I said, under my breath.

Kip looked outraged, but he kept quiet.

"So, it is with great pleasure," said Mr. Caparelli, "that I announce the winner of the Hope Springs Comedy contest: Ms. Samantha Reynolds! For a musical comedy version of that classic fairy tale, *Rumpelstiltskin*!"

Not Fair

My stomach dropped like an elevator. Some people clapped politely, but not me. Samantha pumped the air a couple of times with her fist, then looked sheepish. A few girls said, "Way to go, Samantha," though not like they really meant it. I was almost afraid to look at Kip, but he had turned away and was rummaging in his backpack. Then everyone was talking at once.

I raised my hand. "Hey, how come nobody ever said the play had to be for a big cast?"

Mr. Caparelli quieted the crowd. "As I explained earlier, before we started reading the scripts, we decided to keep an eye out for a good play with a big cast. Mind you, that doesn't mean we weren't going to seriously consider the plays with smaller casts."

But you *didn't*, I thought, fuming.

Mr. Caparelli continued. "I understand that sometimes in the past, additions have been made to the cast after the winner was chosen. But Samantha has managed to come up with an ingenious idea for cast expansion all on her own." He was clearly excited. It was clearly unfair.

"And isn't she just the smartest little kiss-ass in the whole world?"

Kip and I turned to see José sitting behind us.

"And what's with this fairy tale business?" He went on. "Eighth grade is way too old for that stuff."

Kip gave a sort of miserable shrug.

All around us everyone was talking about the subject of the play. *A fairy tale?*

Lyndsey Ching—one of the few Populars in the room—raised her hand. "Mr. Caparelli . . ."

"Most kids call me Mr. C.," said the director.

"Okay, whatever," said Lyndsey. "Mr. C., are we actually going to do that story about the weird little guy who stamps a hole in the ground when some girl guesses his name?"

"That's only part of it!" said Theodore "*Mr. C.*" Caparelli, with a broad smile. "Don't forget, Rumpelstiltskin helps that girl by spinning huge piles of straw into gold. Samantha has come up with some dynamite songs, most with tunes you'll recognize."

José leaned over to us again. "I bet it's not going to be

the *real* version," he whispered, "where Rumpelstiltskin stamps so hard he gets his foot caught in a crack in the earth and is split in half. Now *that* would be sweet—but hard to perform more than once."

In any other circumstances, I would have laughed. But it was all starting to sink in. "Who cares? This is still a little kids' story," I whispered back angrily. Kip was hugging his backpack and glowering at Mr. C. "And she's made it into a *musical?*" I added. "Makes no sense. What would we sing about?"

The Sweet Tooth of Death or Forget It

I couldn't even *begin* to do homework that night. I called Kip. "I'm still fried about this *Rumpelstiltskin* joke winning," I said.

"It still sucks, doesn't it?" said Kip quietly. I could hardly hear him.

"So, are you okay?"

"If you mean has anyone called to say it was all a big joke and I won after all, the answer's no." At least he was upping his volume now.

"I'm ready to let off a stink bomb in Caparelli's office," I said. "Even if he wasn't the only one who picked the winner."

"So are you going to the audition tomorrow?" Kip asked.

"Audition?" I said. "Are you nuts?"

"But this was going to be your Big Year, trying for a leading part, remember?" argued Kip.

"Yeah, but in *your* play, not some stupid excuse for a musical written by the number-one class Geek. I want to be in *The Sweet Tooth of Death* or forget it."

That night, I couldn't get to sleep. I wasn't sure where this tossing and turning was coming from—Kip losing or me not acting. Being in the annual play had been my favorite part of middle school—actually, about the only part I could stand. I finally dozed off, trying to remember the story of Rumpelstiltskin and wondering again what we could possibly sing about.

—

Pick a Number

I was pouring milk on my cereal the next morning, when the phone rang.

"This is God speaking. Go to the audition, or Kip will do something awful."

"Okay, okay, get a grip. I'll go to the stupid audition. But I don't have to like it."

"You are permitted not to like it," said Kip, still using his "God" voice. "Just promise me you'll go."

I went. I told myself I was only doing this for Kip. To keep my best friend happy. Besides, I didn't want him to be on my case all year if I *didn't* go.

The crowd was smaller than the day before. There was a definite absence of Goths, and probably anyone who'd been looking to be in a play with a humorous take on death or dismemberment. Of course, not only Populars and Jocks avoided auditions. At least half the school would rather eat rocks than try out for a play. Want people to think you're a Geek or gay? Hang out near the theater.

Still, it's a pretty big school, and some thirty or forty kids were lining up to take a number for their turn to read from the script and sing. I was glad to see Rusty and José there, especially after what José had said the day before. Obviously he was like me—better any play than no play.

Ms. Lopez, our music teacher, taught us all a few lines from an extremely goofy song called "We Are So Unimportant." This was what everyone would be singing during the audition. The tune sounded vaguely like "The Hokey Pokey." It was sung by the Miller and his daughter, Daffodil, who would later have to do the bit with the straw or lose her head. Ms. Lopez explained that this pair of peasants basically wants to be rich and famous.

I had gone to the audition without Kip. No surprise there. I've never been able to talk him into auditioning for anything, so he wouldn't have tried out, even if he had won.

"I don't mind acting for friends," Kip always said, "but no way am I doing anything in front of the whole school."

I got in line to pick a number from a box. I was still

sort of in shock that I was not going to be Detective Slade. That *nobody* was. I reminded myself I was auditioning just to get Kip off my back. I'd try out for laughs. I probably wouldn't even get a part.

Actually, by the time my turn rolled around, I was this close to leaving. Samantha, who was there to audition for her own play—how strange is that?—had just come up to me. She was wearing her usual weird combination of clothing—this time it was flowered bellbottoms from a million years ago and an orange striped T-shirt.

"I think it's great you're trying out for my play," she said. "You're the best actor in this school. I am *not* kidding."

"Thanks," I said. I gave her a sort of fake smile and looked around nervously, wondering who else had heard her. No matter what Kip had said, I felt like I was being disloyal to him—talking to the enemy or something. Trying out for the enemy's stupid play.

"Number 22," called out Mr. Caparelli.

And I stepped up to the piano.

—

Sooooo Unimportant

Girls picked numbers from a separate box. Lyndsey Ching, the Popular from my English class, was number 22, same as me. First, we each had to sing solo on the part we'd learned; then we sang it a couple of times together. It bugged me how the kids who went before us seemed to have forgotten that this was supposed to be a comedy and were acting like it was some Shakespearean tragedy. I decided to really cut loose and make the Miller as obnoxious as I could.

I swaggered around, puffing out my chest and trying to make my voice sound like a pompous nitwit. The part went like this:

Miller and Daffodil: *We are soooooo unimportant and life shouldn't be this way. We are soooooo unimportant and it's like this every day.*

Miller: *If I ever get some money,*

Daffodil: *If I ever can be cool,*

Miller and Daffodil: *We'll be ever soooooo important, and all other folks will drool.*

Lyndsey got into the spirit of it right away, and on our second run-through, did this great Valley Girl imitation on *If I ever can be cool.*

But, "Thank you, Topher. Thank you, Lyndsey," was all Mr. C. said.

"Next?" said Ms. Lopez.

And that was that.

Bad Daniel

Dashing out of school, I almost ran into Daniel Brickster—"Bad Daniel," as some kids had called him in first grade, to distinguish him from another Daniel. He was hanging out near the bus stop with a couple of his socks-for-brains Jock friends.

"Hey T-Man," said Daniel. "Where'd you get those shoes? Bargain Box?" The socks-for-brains got a laugh out of that one. Probably paid to laugh, I thought bitterly.

"No, but I bet they have some there in your size," was all I had in the way of a comeback. Dumb.

Why didn't life give you some warning when a Loser like Daniel was lurking nearby?

—

Skinny Cat on Drugs

I felt totally wiped when I got home. I collapsed on the living room floor, letting Button walk on my stomach and then curl up by my face, purring loudly. I heard a familiar thumping sound, and, sure enough, my ten-year-old sister came pounding through the living room on all fours. She leaped over me and Button, who jumped off by first digging his claws into my chest.

"Quit that galloping," I moaned, rubbing my scratched chest. "You're not a horse."

"I'm not galloping," panted Molly, rounding the sofa and leaping over the footstool. "I'm cantering. There's a huge difference." She circled the living room three more times and disappeared into her room.

I rolled over and almost squashed Button, now lying right next to me. He was always getting tripped over, or his tail stepped on, because we didn't know he was there. He'd be eyeballing a blue jay from the window, making that weird throat noise cats make when they watch birds, and the next thing you knew, he was racing in front of you, chasing some unseen prey. It would seem like only a second later you'd turn around to find him sacked out, right where you were about to sit.

There was a lot less chasing these days, though. Button had diabetes, and it was making him skinny, thirsty, and tired. His soft, orange hair was now dull and sort of bunchy. It kind of reminded me of this old fake fur coat someone had worn in last year's play.

Button got insulin shots twice a day from Mom or Dad. He never complained. Mom said that's because the shots don't hurt him, but I think it's because he's brave. I know I hate getting *one* shot, much less two a day. The vet had said the shots might keep Button going for a couple more years. Or less. You never could tell with cats. I hoped they kept him going forever or until he was really old, not just ten, which is supposed to be like seventy in people years. My grandparents are way older than that and nobody's giving *them* shots.

—

MR. C. ASSIGNS the ROLES

I was really surprised to see Kip waiting for me outside the theater.

"Hey, I couldn't stay away," he said. "I'm just a glutton for punishment. Plus, I want to be here when you get a big part."

"Well, you'll be disappointed, because there's no way

I'll get one, especially the way I was messing around at the audition," I said, as we got seats toward the back.

"But you want one, don't you?" grinned Kip. "Or you wouldn't have told me that eleven times already since the audition."

I swatted at Kip with my cap, and he laughed and ducked, and then Mr. Caparelli was clapping his hands and announcing loudly, "Quiet, please! You can't hear the part you got if you're talking."

Everyone hushed up as Mr. C. started reading from his clipboard.

"Here are the principal roles." He held up his free hand, like a traffic cop. "And keep quiet till I'm through. In order of appearance: The part of the Narrator will be played by Samantha Reynolds."

(Good, I thought, I didn't want that one—all reading, no acting.)

"The two Guards will be played by Michael O'Neil and Neesha Brooks."

(Okay, so much for the smallest parts.)

"The Miller will be played by José Santiago."

(Rats, that would have been a fun part. Well, there was always the King.)

"The Miller's daughter, Daffodil, will be Lyndsey Ching."

(Good choice, but she's no "daffodil" with that black hair.)

"The King will be Rusty Jackson."

(No fair! That had to be the best part. I bet Rusty got it because he's so big.)

Mr. Caparelli paused dramatically. "And the part of Rumpelstiltskin will be performed by . . . Topher Blakely."

Everyone turned around and stared at me. "Way to go!" said Kip, offering a high five. I felt my ears get hot. I'd gotten my wish—a big part—but *this* part? And in *this* play?

Mr. Caparelli was not done. "Everyone else will have a part in the chorus," he said, spreading his arms wide. "And the chorus will be the Straw!"

—

Mean Guy With a Fake Beard

We all lined up to get a script and a CD of the music. Mr. C. and Ms. Lopez had recorded themselves singing all the songs and had burned CDs so everyone could learn the music. I overheard a good deal of grumbling going on from the Straw kids.

"We have to spend half our time flopped in a pile on top of each other. Like is that supposed to be *dancing?*"

"How are we going to change from a Straw costume into a Gold one right there on stage? This is so not making any sense."

I felt sorry for them, but suddenly this glossy color image of me taking a bow popped into my head. I wouldn't get to be Detective Slade, but a mean guy with a fake beard was actually kind of cool. I could really see myself in the part.

Except for one thing that had me puzzled. I waited for a chance to talk to Mr. Caparelli alone. "Isn't Rumpelstiltskin supposed to be like a gnome-sized guy?"

"Oh, yes," said Mr. C. "We did consider that you *are* a bit tall for the part, but you'll do fine. Try hunching over and squatting down as much as possible." He hunched over and sort of waddled around like a duck. "Here, you try it," he said. Several kids were watching and started cracking up.

"Yeah, um, I think I get it. Maybe later," I mumbled. No color shots of bowing now.

—

Kip Explains

"You *are* too tall, but I bet I know why he picked you," Kip said on the way home. "Joey Black is the right size, but he can't sing, and Brittani is the right size and can sing, but a girl—especially a *Popular*—might not agree to wear a fake beard and be a mean little man."

"I like the idea of a fake beard and being mean," I told him. "But hunching over and singing at the same time sounds really hard. Plus, it's got huge dork potential."

—

Are You Nuts?

It turned out the hunching-over part was not as bad as the singing. I had told my family I was going to have a leading part in the new play, but I didn't tell them much else. Now here I was, setting the table for supper and listening to "Stop That Crying," from Act I, on my headset. It would be my first solo, set to the tune of "Itsy Bitsy Spider," and featured the refrain:

> *Stop that crying, foolish girl,*
> *Stop that crying now!*
> *I can't stand the sound of sobs*
> *And tears, you snuffling cow.*

Talk about awful. I started groaning and making faces, slamming down the silverware.

"What are you *listening* to?" asked Molly. She was carrying two glasses of milk and seemed hesitant to come near the table.

"*Rumpelstiltskin, the Musical.*" I pointed a finger-gun to my head and fired.

"Put it on our player so we can all hear it," said Dad, as we sat down to eat.

"Yes, let's hear it, honey!" Mom added, just to make things worse.

I rolled my eyes, but did as I was told. I know these people. They won't give up until I give in. They have so little respect for a person's privacy. Soon the *oom-pahs* of "Stop That Crying" could just be heard coming from the speakers.

"Louder than that, Topher," said my mom. "We can barely hear it."

I sighed and cranked up the volume.

"Sounds kind of like an angry polka," commented my dad, after a bit.

"Sounds like you get to be a real jerk," said Molly cheerfully.

That did it. I turned off the CD player and slapped the script down on the table. "We all get to be jerks," I said. "Jerks and dorks. Just look at this list of songs."

Molly read the first page out loud.

RUMPELSTILTSKIN

A musical in two acts, by Samantha Reynolds

Cast, in order of appearance:

Narrator

Miller

Daffodil

Guard 1

Guard 2

King

Straw/Gold

Rumpelstiltskin

SONGS:

Act I:

We Are So Unimportant... Miller and Daffodil

Tell the King (About My Talented Girl)... Miller, Soldiers

Let's See Some Gold (or It's off With Your Head)... King

Woe Is Me... Daffodil

Everyone burst out laughing. Except me.

"This is great!" said Mom. "What a hoot! Samantha always was a talented kid."

"Talented?" I said. "More like a teacher's-pet-brainiac kid." I had a real urge to smack someone. "Well, I'm glad you all think it's so funny. Because I think it's pathetic and we'll be made fun of for the next fifty years."

"Oh, come on, T, this'll be fun," said Dad. "If the songs are anything like their titles, I bet you'll have audiences howling with laughter."

I pulled at my hair. "Aaackk!" Could they be any more hopeless? Slowly, since I was explaining this to very simple minds, I said, "You don't get it. You think everyone who comes to this show will see how it's supposed to be funny. But it won't just be adults with a sense of humor, or little kids who like fairy tales who'll show up. Anyone can come. All ages. And a lot of them won't think it's funny, they'll think it's dorky. They'll laugh all right, but not the way you will. They'll laugh us right off the stage, I just know it. And they'll keep laughing till they graduate. Maybe forever."

I was on a roll now. "And then they'll think of some dumb nickname, like 'Rumpy' or 'Stumbleskin,' and they'll call me that all through high school. And I'll be so miserable I'll turn to drugs and never do my homework and never get into college and end up working at Taco Bell for the rest of my life."

I paused for breath. All of them were staring at me.

My dad smiled. "All that for being Rumpelstiltskin?"

"Why don't you just quit?" asked Molly.

"And miss being the male lead in a play?" I said. "Are you nuts?"

How Sad Can My Life Be?

After English, I was surprised to see Lyndsey Ching break away from her cluster of Queen Bees and Wannabees and walk over to me. "Did you listen to that whole CD?" She asked.

"Yeah," I said. "My family thought it was funny. I don't get it. I think it's stupid."

"Some of the songs are just weird, you know?" said Lyndsey, adjusting her shiny black ponytail. "You know my solo, 'Woe Is Me'? Well, check this out." And Lyndsey sort of whisper-sang under her breath:

Oh woe, ah woe, ah woe.

How low can my heart go?

Oh woe, ah woe is me,

How sad can my life be?

"Sorry," I said, "But that's nothing compared to where I have to sing . . .

I can spin that straw to gold—

A piece of cake, a spree.

But first you have to show what you

Can give of yours to me.

"Can't you just *hear* Daniel Brickster and his Loser pals making that into a dirty joke?"

Lyndsey winced. "Yeah, glad I don't have anything like that. At least I don't *think* I do. But do you realize you call me a *cow* in this play? At least I get to call you a 'nasty wicked baby stealer.'"

Kip joined us as we headed for the cafeteria line. I couldn't believe Lyndsey was still with us. I could see her friends in line up ahead, looking back like they couldn't believe it, either.

"Your play is so much better than this one," I told Kip. "Plus, it's a great mystery. Everyone knows how this fairy tale ends. There won't be any surprises. And I seriously doubt Mr. C. can pull it off."

Rusty pushed into line, waving his copy of the script. "Make way for the king! Better give me cuts," he said. "Check it out. I bet I get to wear a crown and a cape and wave a sword around and threaten people with it. I am already feeling the power."

"Oh, great," said Lyndsey. "And I have to marry him. I mean stupid Daffodil does. It's sexist, is what it is. Why would Samantha write something like this?"

"It's just a fairy tale," said Rusty. "And it's supposed to be silly. Don't get all political about it, Lyndsey."

First Day of Rehearsal

The theater was being used for something else, so the whole cast met in the gym right after school. It was raining and the air indoors was damp, smelling of armpits, dirty socks, and Brittani Nelson's perfume. Mr. Caparelli divided us into groups to practice separately. The Straw was in the center of the room with Mr. Beach, the P.E. teacher, learning dance steps. The Miller, the King, the Guards, and the Narrator were with Mr. C. at one end of the gym. Lyndsey and I met at the other, with Ms. Lopez and an electric keyboard.

First we had to do these embarrassing voice warm-ups, where we had to go "La, la, la, lee, lee, lee, loo, loo, loo . . ."

That finally was over, and Ms. Lopez said, "We will start with your big duet in Act II. It's 'Hand Over the Babe,' and it's the part in the story where Rumpelstiltskin comes back to demand payment for having spun all that straw into gold for Daffodil a year earlier."

She handed us sheets of music and started playing the song and singing. She's got this distinctive, high voice that I remembered from the CD. It was hard to pay attention to her because I kept trying to remember who she reminded me of. Someone on TV?

"Now, you try it," said Ms. Lopez. "Topher, the song starts right after Daffodil says, *Oh, you surprised me, Little Man! Whatever do you want?*"

Bam. All at once it's performance time. I cleared my throat and began:

I'm back like I promised, I'm back here, I say.
Now give me that baby, your debt to repay.

Then Lyndsey sang:

My baby? You're joking! Give my baby to you?
Now be off! Just vamoose, take a hike, get
* a clue!*

Ms. Lopez interrupted here. "Don't forget to sound fierce, Topher dear," she said, with her special sugar smile. "And Lyndsey, remember Daffodil's anger will build as the song goes along. You aren't mad yet, you're laughing at him."

The gym was getting hotter and stuffier and noisier by the minute. Lyndsey and I struggled through the rest of the song, with Ms. Lopez interrupting way too much. The tune was hard to learn—it was one of the few Samantha had made up. Most of the songs had familiar tunes—Christmas carols, nursery rhymes, a few recent rock hits, and one that sounded a lot like the high school fight song. But "Hand Over the Babe" was one of her very own compositions.

"I can't sound fierce with a tune this weird," I finally said. "It's too hard." I fully expected to be reminded for the umpteenth time of Samantha's talent, but Ms. Lopez surprised me.

"Some changes may have to be made. Samantha will work with us, particularly at early rehearsals, in case we need to make adjustments to the music."

That sounded good to me, but apparently there wasn't going to be any adjusting today. Ms. Lopez had us go over and over the song. I got to feeling nervous and bored at the same time. Next, Ms. Lopez sang, interrupting herself to talk about the right way to breathe. I was pretty sure there wasn't enough air in the gym to breathe normally, much less "from the diaphragm."

It was also hard to pay attention because I kept being distracted by the Straw. They were practicing their dance steps with Mr. Beach, doing a lot of arm waving and spinning around and falling down, laughing, when they got dizzy—which happened a lot.

"Topher! Pay attention!" I jerked my eyes and brain back to Ms. Lopez. Lyndsey was giving me a disgusted look. "Now what was I just saying about projecting your voice?" asked Ms. Lopez, sugar smile returning.

"Don't do it?" I guessed.

"No!" said Ms. Lopez. "*Do* do it. You have to sing so everyone in the theater can hear you, even those in the back row. Now listen to me once more." And she sang:

Hand it over now, Queenie, give the babe there
  to me.
You must keep your promise, or sorry you'll be.

Oh, man, all of a sudden I remembered who her voice reminded me of—Miss Piggy, on those old *Muppets Show* reruns. Unfortunately, figuring this out didn't help in the paying-attention department. In fact, I started to crack up, tried to stop, and got the hiccups. But at least I wasn't bored anymore.

—

Is It Already Rehearsal #9?

"I really do *not* feel ready for this," I told Lyndsey when I got to rehearsal. It was to be the first run-through of Act I.

"Didn't you practice?" she asked, in this annoying I-practice-even-in-my-sleep sort of voice. There was more than a little bit of the Study Geek lurking in this Popular.

"Yes, of course I practiced!" It was almost true—close enough. I had looked at my lines some on the bus, except Rusty kept interrupting me with his jokes. "Also, there was this report for history class," I told Lyndsey, "that I'd sort of forgotten about until Sunday afternoon. At least I remembered it then, which should count for something, right? But, of course, it turns out that absolutely *no* libraries are open on Sunday afternoon and I had to get everything off the Internet. But for some reason, my parents said Molly got to use the computer *first* for her state report on North Dakota or North somewhere, even though my homework is much harder and the baby gets whatever she wants. And then we have this lame dial-up modem that takes a gazillion years to download anything, so I had to stay up really late doing it, and my mom wouldn't call in an excuse for me to miss first period. So I am unbelievably tired and—"

"Something's wrong with your *mute* button," interrupted Lyndsey. She had been making a gesture like someone trying to press a button on a remote control.

"Ha, Ha," I said. "You'd understand if you had a little sister."

"But I don't," said Lyndsey. And she walked off to join Neesha.

When rehearsal started, I tried looking over the script while José, Rusty, and the others went through the first three scenes.

Scene four began with eight members of the Straw all bunched together on the floor, curled up in turtlelike positions, waiting to be spun into gold. Lyndsey sang, "Woe Is Me." Like "Hand Over the Babe," this tune was one of Samantha's own originals. Occasionally Lyndsey got the notes wrong and would try to start over.

"I'm sorry, Mr. C.," she said. "But this music is just not making sense to me."

I saw her look over at Samantha (not hard to spot in a bright green tank top and floppy yellow pants), who was discussing something with Ms. Lopez by the piano. If Samantha had heard, she didn't let it show.

"Don't worry, you'll get it later," said Mr. Caparelli, gesturing for me to come on stage. He was trying to get through the whole act without interruptions.

"But, Mr. Caparelli," Lyndsey persisted, "couldn't the music be changed to make it less—"

Mr. Caparelli cut her off. "Your entrance, Rumpelstiltskin. Quick, quick!"

Queen Bees are not used to being cut off in mid-sentence. Lyndsey looked royally fried.

I hunched over, clutching my script, and sort of waddled over to Lyndsey. She was seated near the Straw, pretending to cry, looking more real-angry than fake-sad. Of course, it didn't help that various members of the Straw kept twitching and whispering. I tried to look right at Lyndsey without looking at the Straw.

"*Stop that crying!*" I said, working on making my voice deep and gruff. "*I hate crying.*"

"*Oh, my! Who are you?*" asked Lyndsey.

"*Not important. Just quit sniveling. What's the matter, anyway?*"

"*Oh, Little Man,*" said Lyndsey, "*My father told the king I can spin straw into gold. I can't. Nobody can. But I have to do it by morning or the king will chop off my head.*"

"Hmmm," I said. "Hmmm." And then "Hmmm," I said

again. I'd paid so much attention to not looking at the Straw that I'd lost my place. I searched the script, turning pages, saying "Hmmm" a few more times. Would Mr. C. start yelling at me? Lyndsey was fuming, blades of Straw were sniggering. Phew, there it was. *"What will you give me to spin all this straw into gold?"*

"You?" said Lyndsey, and she laughed. She actually made it sound like a real laugh, like she thought it was a ridiculous idea.

I felt my face get all hot. *"Yeah, me! Who else is going to bail you out here?"*

Louder giggles from the Straw pile.

"All right, you may try," said Lyndsey, as if she were doing me some huge favor.

I glared at her. *"What will you give me to spin all of this miserable straw into gold?"*

"My necklace?" Now Lyndsey sounded a bit more like Daffodil, the poor miller's daughter, and less like Lyndsey, the ticked-off kid.

"Very well," I growled, gesturing for her to move so I could sit by the spinning wheel. Somehow I aimed my left arm too close to Lyndsey and accidentally pushed her right off the chair.

"Hey!" yelled Lyndsey, no longer being Daffodil.

"Oops!" I said, no longer being Rumpelstiltskin. I held out my hand to help her up, but she jumped up on her own, glaring at me.

Now It's Rehearsal #12

"Everyone, listen up!" Mr. Caparelli was trying to get the chattering Straw to pay attention. "The scene today starts with Daffodil trying to stay awake to see how the strange little man is going to spin straw into gold, but she isn't able to keep her eyes open."

Of course, right away I had to wrinkle up my nose, cross my eyes, and stick out my tongue so I'd look "strange." Rusty laughed and Mr. C. put check marks by our names on his clipboard cast list. He had started to keep track of people who were goofing around, not paying attention, and generally pissing him off. Three checks and you got a warning. Five and you were out of the play.

How many checks did I have? Not that I wanted to get thrown out of the play, but I wouldn't mind being considered Trouble once in a while. It would be sort of cool.

The scene got going and Lyndsey did a good job of yawning, slowly sinking to the floor and closing her eyes. I stayed on the bench, pretending to twirl a spinning wheel and moving my hands like I'd seen TV magicians do, to look like I was doing some magic. The Straw stood up, one by one, twirling in circles to the music Ms. Lopez was playing.

To pretend they were being turned into gold, each

member of the Straw was supposed to pull off the straw-colored outer costume to reveal a gold-colored costume underneath. Since there were no costumes yet, they moved their arms to show they were doing this, and then sang "We Were Straw, But Now We're Gold." Although the tune was "Old MacDonald Had a Farm," it seemed to come out a bit differently for each piece of Straw. Ms. Lopez said it was fine for now.

"You will be working on this a great deal in the weeks ahead," she reminded them kindly.

—

WHY IS THIS SO HARD?

The rehearsal ran late. "You will have to pay more attention to my stage directions, Cast," said Mr. C., before dismissing us. "It's hard to do if you're reading from the script. It's even harder if you've left your script at home." He glared at Michael, who had remembered to bring his script only about four times. "*Everyone* have your lines memorized by Monday. Understand?"

I understood, all right. And I figured I wasn't the only one, from all the groans and whines of "No fair!"

I went up to Lyndsey as she was loading her backpack. "Want to go over lines with me sometime this weekend?" I asked. I felt my cheeks get hot. It had come out sounding like I was asking for a date.

"Uh, sure, why not?" Lyndsey said. She glanced over her shoulder.

Was I paranoid, or was she looking around to see if any of her friends were watching her talk to a borderline Geek? Like they'd be hanging around the theater ever.

"But it can't be at my house," she added. "My parents are having it painted and it's a mess everywhere. They said no guests."

"We can do it at mine," I told her. "How about Saturday at 10:00?" I was careful to pick a time when Molly would be riding at the ranch. If a girl came over to the house to see me, for *any* reason, I knew I would never hear the end of it from Molly.

Lyndsey took a deep breath. "Okay," she said. "Your house tomorrow at 10:00. Here, write down your address." I started to write it on a scrap of paper, when Lyndsey added, "Unless you have cats. I'm allergic to cats. I start sneezing and my eyes swell up."

"We have a cat," I said, crumpling up the paper. "And his hair is everywhere." Why was this so hard? We had to practice together. All our scenes were together.

Lyndsey shrugged. "Maybe you can come over to my house next week when the painting's over." She picked up her pack and headed for the door.

I sat slumped in my seat on the way home on the bus, not saying anything.

"What's with you?" asked Kip. "I'm the one who gets to be bummed about my play losing."

"It didn't lose," I grumbled. "It just didn't win."

Kip rolled his eyes. "Thank you, Mr. Positive Feedback."

"Listen," I said, sitting up and leaning closer to him. "I know this is going to sound weird, but would you help me practice my lines this weekend? We have to have them memorized by Monday and I've got a ton to learn."

Kip gave me a look. "Wait a sec. I'm all for you being in this play, since mine's out, but help you learn *lines* for it? That's a real stretch."

"Never mind," I said. "Just forget it." I slumped back down. "I'll get my dad or mom to help."

"Not parents," groaned Kip. "That's the worst. What's wrong with Lyndsey? Isn't she in all your scenes? Or is she too cool to practice with you?"

"Button's what's wrong," I told him. "He'll make her sneeze and swell up."

"Like a balloon? Like the girl in *Willy Wonka*?" Kip laughed. I had to laugh, too, picturing Lyndsey sneezing and floating helplessly up to our living room ceiling.

"What if I help you with math or something?" I asked. "Please?"

"Oh, okay," said Kip. "I've got a test coming up next week and it's all stuff you know."

—

A Funny Daffodil

I got Kip to come over to my house on Sunday afternoon.

"Lines first, then we do your math," I told him.

Actually, "first" turned out to be him spending a nanosecond looking at the script and then ranting about how he couldn't believe this play had beaten his and how he could have set *The Sweet Tooth of Death* to tunes from *Sesame Street* and made a bunch of knives dance, if he'd known that's what it took to win. Something nuts like that.

Finally he calmed down and we got to work on the scene that was the climax of the play. This is where the Miller's daughter, Daffodil ("the dippy Daffodil," as Kip started calling her), supposedly guesses Rumpelstiltskin's name. In this big fury, he stomps a hole in the ground, falls in, and disappears forever.

I started with my lines, "*Well, my pretty, you may as well save us both time and hand over the babe. You will never guess my name. Not in a million tries!*" I was bent over next to Kip, pulling on my imaginary beard and giving a raspy laugh.

"What are you *doing?*" asked Kip.

This was not Daffodil's first line.

"I'm 'chuckling in an evil manner,' like it says in the script," I told him, still hunched over.

Kip rolled his eyes. Then, clasping his hands, he read in this high, fake-sweet voice, "*Oh do let me at least try. After all, you said I could have three more guesses.*"

"*Okay, okay, get on with it,*" I said, working on my grumbly, low, Rumpelstiltskin voice.

"*Is it . . . Snookums?*" Kip's Daffodil sounded perky and truly brainless.

"*Good grief, no.*"

"*Is it . . . Pointynose?*" Kip touched my nose ever so lightly with the tip of his finger.

"*No! Come on, hand it over.*" I did some more evil chuckling, but it was getting hard—Kip was being very funny.

Kip opened his eyes very wide. "*Is it . . . Rum—pel—stilt—skin?*"

Here I jumped up, waving my arms as wildly as I could. "*Who told you? Who told you? You cheated! I know you did!*"

Kip put his hand to his chest, like he's all indignant and innocent and stuff, gave me this shocked look, and said, "*My dear little man, I don't know what you mean, I'm sure.*"

I laughed so hard I collapsed to the floor. "I can't do it," I finally panted, wiping tears from my eyes. "Don't be such a funny Daffodil. Let's try again."

But it was no use. Every time we got to the part about "my dear little man," I could not act mad and stomp. Matter of fact, I couldn't even stay standing. Finally, we bagged that scene and decided to practice another one.

"Don't take this the wrong way, but you're really good," I said to Kip, when we were having a break and a snack in the kitchen.

Kip got all red, but he looked pleased. "Well it's easy

here," he said. "It's not the same as being on a real stage."

"I still wish you were in the play," I said. "And you have a most excellent singing voice." That got us laughing all over again.

Button wandered in and sniffed around the cuffs of Kip's pants. "How's he doing these days?" asked Kip, leaning over to scratch the kitty's bony back.

"Okay, I guess. I think he's starting to eat more and he hangs around us, getting in the way like any normal cat. So that's got to be a good sign."

We decided to work on a scene at the beginning of Act II, when Rumpelstiltskin first shows up to demand baby payment and the queen refuses to hand it over. Daffodil was saying, "*But surely there is something else you'd like. How about my crown? Or my throne? I've got buckets of jewels now—take those! But not my baby!*"

I tried the next lines from memory. "*No way! What do I need with riches? Give me the baby. I spun that straw into gold and saved your neck. Head. Whatever. This baby is mine! I kept my part of the bargain, pointless miller's kid, and so should you!*" It didn't sound right. I looked at Kip. "Is that it?"

"No, it's 'worthless miller's brat, and now you must keep yours.'"

"Okay, '*worthless miller's brat, and now you must—*'" I stopped. I had just noticed something. "Wait a sec. You just corrected me without looking at the script. Have you *memorized* this? I know you have a great memory, but you just saw it for the first time today, right?"

Kip shrugged. "It's just something I can do," he said.

—

Focus!

I was feeling pretty confident the next day at the start of rehearsal. I have *got* to learn not to do that. Of course things didn't go well. Although I had memorized more lines than most people, there was still no way I could get through the stomping scene without cracking up. Even with Lyndsey saying her own Daffodil lines and Mr. Caparelli and all the cast watching, this picture kept popping into my head of Kip doing those lines, and I'd lose it.

Mr. Caparelli did not crack up. Not even a little. "Focus, Topher!" he kept saying. "Stay in character. Please! Now once more, from 'well my pretty . . . '"

And we'd try again. Finally I could get through the scene, but I was trying so hard to remember my lines and not think of Kip at the same time that I couldn't get into being this angry Rumpelstiltskin guy. Even the part I loved, the floor stomping, was really lame.

"Topher," said Mr. Caparelli. "You've got to pump up the scene. Rumpelstiltskin here is surprised, disappointed, and—most of all—furious. Go over the top with it."

—

Thanks to Tom and Jerry

Samantha started scene seven with the Narrator's words, *"In the morning, when Daffodil opened her eyes, all the straw was gone, and in its place stood a tall pile of gold coins. The mysterious little man had disappeared."*

"Oh, my goodness!" exclaimed Lyndsey as Daffodil, sitting up and clapping her hands against her cheeks.

At this cue, Rusty-the-King threw open an imaginary door and came bounding onstage, waving his arms and roaring, *"Show—me—the—gold!"*

Daffodil pointed dramatically at the pile of Gold, formerly the Straw, now standing tightly packed together, with raised arms and smiling faces, trying to look shiny. The King did an exaggerated double take, and jumped back. I recognized that move from several *Tom and Jerry* cartoons.

The King then danced around the gold, rubbing his hands and saying, "Oh, yummy, yummy, yummy, money, money, money!"

"Excuse me, that's not in the script, Mr. C.," complained Samantha.

"Stick to the script, King," Mr. C. said quickly. He and Mr. Beach were watching the scene intently.

King Rusty was now launching into his song, "A Miracle—I Must See More," sung to the tune of "Mary Had a Little Lamb."

Partway through, Mr. Beach stopped him. "Too static. I want you to take Daffodil's hands, and both of you skip around in a circle as you sing this. Action keeps the story from coming to a screeching halt during a song."

Ms. Lopez took it from the top, and this time, Rusty grabbed Lyndsey's hands, skipping around with her in ever-faster circles as he sang. He put a lot of energy into it. All those repeated "must see mores" were sounding like "muss Seymour" to me.

Lyndsey appeared to be keeping up until the end of the song, when Rusty, who was a big guy, let go and she shot off to one side, like a skater in crack-the-whip. She staggered against the Gold before regaining her balance and composure. The Gold forgot gold doesn't talk, and said, "Watch it!" and "Hey!" before being shushed by Mr. C.

"*Guards!*" shouted the King. "*Bring this brilliant girl another, bigger pile of straw!*" He turned and smiled at Daffodil, raising one eyebrow and cocking an imaginary crown to one side of his head. "*I'll be back in the morning. Spin all this into gold and you shall be my queen. If not, it's off with your head. Nothing personal, of course.*"

"*Yes, your Royal Most Highness,*" said Daffodil, clenching her fists.

"Mr. C.," interrupted Samantha. "Daffodil is supposed to be scared, not angry."

"Yes, please show us a scared and worried Daffodil, Lyndsey," said Mr. Caparelli, but this time he didn't even look at Samantha.

I whispered to José, who was standing with me offstage. "Think Mr. C. is getting a little tired of Samantha's comments?"

"Why *would* he?" José whispered back, mimicking Samantha's frown and crossed arms.

I tried not to laugh, but it came out anyway—in a snort, which I tried to turn into a cough. When I looked back at the stage, Samantha was glaring at me.

King Rusty marched off the stage, followed by the Guards, who held their arms out, encircling the Gold, pretending to carry it away.

"Twirl as you leave, to add to the sparkle, but stay close together," instructed Mr. Beach. This was more than most of the Gold could handle—"Hey, that's my foot;" "Stop hitting me, jerk!"—and once again, we were treated to the unexpected magic of talking gold.

After rehearsal, we all met in the auditorium seats for notes. This was the time Mr. C., Ms. Lopez, and Mr. Beach all made comments about how the rehearsal had gone. They pointed out which scenes had gone well and which parts needed work. Being both the playwright and the Narrator, Samantha was in the odd position of being someone to give *and* to get notes. She started right in complaining about Rusty adding his own words and Lyndsey being angry instead of scared.

Mr. C. agreed. "Follow the script, people. Rusty, stick with your lines. Lyndsey, you can give this your own spin, but you can't change your character. Daffodil is shallow but rightfully scared. Stick to that."

Samantha stood with her arms crossed again and said

she hoped nobody *else* was going to start changing their part. She said it was *her* play, after all.

Lyndsey said nothing, but she looked mad.

—

WOBBLY STRAW AT REHEARSAL #18

"Where is everybody?" I asked. The auditorium looked almost empty.

"The Straw is practicing in the gym," said Samantha. "With their two cheerleaders."

"We're going to have Straw that does *cheers?*" It seemed like a stretch, even for this play.

"Hey, like this?" asked Rusty, and he began punching the air and kicking his legs. "We're the Straw and we don't care, so we'll turn to Gold . . . um . . ."

". . . in our underwear!" I finished. I imagined the Straw doing cartwheels. I found myself wondering—was it possible to be upstaged by *straw?*

The Straw came in with Mr. Beach, led by Brittani and Caitlyn—Straws who were also cheerleaders. It seemed Mr. Beach had a plan for dealing with the full Straw cast looking unpilelike.

"Places!" called Mr. Caparelli.

Lyndsey sat on the stool that was now in front of the bike-tire spinning wheel and I got ready to hide myself behind the Straw. Only this time, the Straw was forming a pyramid of kids. As I watched, five of the biggest students knelt on the floor, then four got on top of them.

"Steady, Eric."

"Okay, get up, Nikki."

"Ahh! Get your knee out of my back!"

Then three more—

"Careful, Jorge, I'm not kidding."

Then two—

"Omigod omigod omigod . . ."

Then Brittani climbed over them all to the top. The Straw was now a tall pile, but it looked wobbly to me.

I stepped back.

Before they could even start the scene, there were cries of "Don't move!" and "I'm slipping!" Two Straws on the bottom caved, bringing down the whole shrieking pile.

"Ow, my arm!" whimpered Brittani.

"Oooh, did you break it?"

"No. I don't know."

"Okay, so that needs some work," said Mr. Beach. Then he drove Brittani to the hospital.

—

"Fair" Is Not the Issue

Ms. Lopez was waving something as she called for everyone to pipe down. "These are tickets for your show," she announced. "Every member of the cast is required to sell twenty tickets, no exceptions."

Everybody groaned.

"That is so unfair!"

"What if we can't find twenty people?"

"If you don't know twenty people, make some new friends. 'Fair' is not the issue." Ms. Lopez was taking no prisoners. "Remember, this drama program, like all the arts programs, runs on donations. And it makes more sense to raise money by having people appreciate the fine work you do than to ask you to sell wrapping paper or candy."

"We already have to do that," someone grumbled.

"Before you leave, pick up a packet of tickets and flyers and sign this sheet so we know who has them," Ms. Lopez went on, smiling sweetly. "If you're going to be in the production, you must sell all twenty by opening night."

I sighed, trudging out the door with tickets and flyers in my backpack. There are few things I hate as much as selling stuff. And I wasn't in the mood to wait for Rusty, who could sell his own mother if he had to.

"Topher!" It was Mr. Caparelli, catching up with me. "I'd like to make a suggestion."

"About selling tickets?"

"No, you're on your own there," Mr. C. chuckled.

(I bet the *directors* didn't have to sell any tickets.)

"About your portrayal of Rumpelstiltskin," he continued. "I think you're a great choice for the role. But your Rumpelstiltskin seems a bit too upbeat. Too cheerful. When you do him, I want you to picture someone you know who's cranky and all wrapped up in themselves."

"I can think of a few eighth graders who are like that," I said.

"Hmm, yes, I'm sure we both could," said Mr. C. "But I'm thinking some adult would be better."

I thought of all my teachers and how they each acted on bad days. "Yeah, I might be able to come up with someone," I said. "I'll think about it."

On the bus home, though, all I could think about was having to sell the stupid twenty tickets. Never in my life have I earned a single prize for selling the most magazines, candy, or wrapping paper.

But at my stop, I braced myself and decided to go for it. If I could unload at least one ticket before I got to my house, maybe it wouldn't seem so impossible to sell the rest. Maybe.

I knocked on the Newsomes' door and stepped back. Not a moment too soon—the door flew open and Banana bounded out. Little Robbie Newsome was attached to him, clinging to the dog's collar and shouting, "Stop, Nana! You have to stay inside!" I made a grab for Banana, but it was too late. Robbie fell off and the big dog raced down the street.

"Hi, Robbie," I said, helping the five-year-old to his feet. "Is your mom or dad home?"

"My mom is," said Robbie, "but she's on the pot."

"Oh," I said. "Well, I'll come back later. Tell her I'm selling tickets to my school's play, if she wants to buy any. Here." I handed Robbie a flyer advertising the play. "I'm in it, too. I'm Rumpelstiltskin." I smiled modestly, but it was wasted on him.

"No, you're not!" Robbie laughed, not taken in by this obvious lie.

"Well, I pretend to be him in the play," I explained.

Robbie looked at the brochure and frowned. "There aren't any words on this I can read," he said, handing it back. "Want to see our new goldfish?"

"Later," I said. "I gotta try to sell these tickets. Please show this to your mom, okay?" This time I put the flyer on the table by the door. "I'll be back. Bye."

Where next? Most people were still at work. I rang the bell at the Taylors'. No one answered. I waited a while and then rang again. Then I knocked. Finally, I stuck a flyer in the mailbox, and started toward the only place left with a car in the driveway—Mr. Stickle's house.

This was always the house I put off until last. Clutching the tickets and the pile of flyers, I walked up and rang the bell. I could hear the TV. I waited, thought of leaving, reminded myself I wanted to sell just one before I got home. The door opened and there was Mr. Stickle's stubbly white face glaring out at me.

"Yeah? What is it?"

"Hi." I tried to smile. "I'm Christopher Blakely from down the street . . . "

"I know who you are," growled Mr. Stickle, coming out of the house. "What do you want?"

I *wanted* to run, but I said, "I'm selling tickets to my school play. It's a musical version of *Rumpelstiltskin*."

"Aren't you a little old for fairy tales?" he asked, squinting at me.

Ouch. The old fart knew how to hurt. "It's a comedy. It's for all ages." I held out a flyer. It trembled slightly in my hand.

Mr. Stickle frowned at it, much the way Robbie had, and I half expected him to say he couldn't read any of the words. Unlike Robbie, he didn't take it, just stood there with his arms crossed.

"I don't buy stuff at the door. I told your sister that when she came by with candy bars last month. You kids spend all your time trying to get money out of people. I'm sick of it. Now vamoose!" He turned his head and spit into the bushes.

I vamoosed.

Stupid old poop, I thought bitterly, as I walked away. He could've just told me no, thank you. He didn't have to be so mean.

I trudged back to the Newsomes'. This time, Robbie's mom answered the door. Fortunately, she ordered four tickets. Unfortunately, there was a catch.

"I'll order these from you," she said, getting out her checkbook, "but your family has to promise to buy Girl

Scout cookies from Helen next time she sells them. Okay?"

I promised. Anything to get the tickets sold. I thanked her and hurried home. I had to get my homework done and work on my lines. I ran up my steps and then, with my hand on the doorknob, I suddenly thought of Mr. Caparelli's suggestion about finding a model for my part. I smiled. I knew the perfect "cranky adult all wrapped up in himself."

I would be a most convincing Rumpelstiltskin.

—

A Seriously Unwanted Visit

Lunch recess. Kip had gone to science class early and I was sitting alone, happily finishing the last of my pepperoni pizza—the only good food the cafeteria serves—when three guys sat down at my table. It was Bad Daniel and a couple of sixth-grade boys.

"Okay, important lesson in how to tell who's gay," Daniel was saying, like I was some sort of stop on a tour.

"This is Topher. He's an *ahctoor.*" Daniel licked his middle finger and ran it over his eyebrow as he said this. "This is almost too easy. We know Topher is gay because he's not only in a play, it's a musical. All guys in plays are *fags,* but the real *fairies,* the real *queens,* are the ones in musicals. Got that?"

The sixth graders snickered, not looking at me.

"Beat it, Daniel," I said, through gritted teeth.

"Hey, I've got a girlfriend, I don't need to," said Daniel.

I hated myself for turning red. I should have known he would twist anything I said into something dirty. The sixth graders snickered again, but I was willing to bet they didn't know why.

"Where's Kippy?" Daniel went on. "I wanted these guys to see my other favorite example of fag-ness."

I said nothing, wishing I'd left early, too.

"You're not being helpful, T-Man," said Daniel with mock regret, getting up. He reached to take a sip of my milk. "Oops, better not. Got to stay safe." All three of them laughed as they walked off, taking my appetite with them.

—

Short Tempers

Our next rehearsal was pretty ragged. The Straw pyramid idea had gone back to the drawing board, so the full supply of Straw was still struggling to look like a pile and not take up the whole stage. A lot of pushing and complaining had to be hushed up by an increasingly short-tempered Mr. Caparelli.

Lyndsey was supposed to sing a reprise of "Woe Is Me," only sounding even sadder, according to Samantha's stage directions. Lyndsey mixed up lines from this scene and the first two spinning scenes, and I got so confused that the only lines I could think of were from last year's show.

Suddenly Lyndsey threw up her hands, shouting, "This won't work!"

Ms. Lopez stopped the music. Surprised, everyone stared at Lyndsey.

"I know it's not *in the script*, but I think Daffodil would be furious by now. She was told she could marry the king if she got the first job done, and then again after the second, and now he's doing take-backs and demanding a third pile of gold. Besides, it's boring to have her just cry every time she sees straw."

"Yeah," came a voice from the Straw. "And it hurts our feelings!"

Backstage, José and I cracked up. But I had my eye on Mr. C. "Think that last interruption from Miss Daffinatious was too much?"

"You mean, was it the last straw?" José elbowed me. "Get it? The *last straw?*"

I rolled my eyes and watched Mr. C. rub his bald head hard enough to get sparks. "Lyndsey, save it for notes. We will follow the script, understand?"

Lyndsey started the scene by marching around the Straw, peeping in between them and making a face like she was looking for rats. She certainly was not the "desperate and scared" Daffodil of Samantha's stage directions.

"*Little Man? Little Man?*" Lyndsey called. "*Little Man?*" she nearly screamed. "*Are you here?*"

Then she marched back and forth, shaking her fist at

the Straw, and singing, "*Oh, woe a woe a woe, how low can my heart go?*" through clenched teeth. This was supposed to be my cue to enter, interrupt Daffodil's crying, and again spin the Straw into Gold, for a price.

But I was wondering, who does she think she is? I mean, I could see her point, but hadn't Mr. C. just told her to cool it with the angry bit? Besides, tough and crabby was *my* job. I decided to one-up her mood.

Lyndsey continued singing.

> *My life is over, sad to say*
> *I'll never make it through today*
> *This straw will not turn gold*
> *I'll die before I'm . . .*

"Aaackk!" Lyndsey jumped a mile.

I had popped up from behind the Straw, shouting, "*Stop that sniveling!*"

It was a big hit with everyone, even Mr. C., although it took a while for Lyndsey to get on with her next line.

"*Oh, Little Man, you're back!*"

"*That's right, missy. Are you having spinning problems again?*"

This was followed by the deal being made where Daffodil promises to give Rumpelstiltskin her first child if he will just spin the straw into gold this last time. Samantha the Narrator, still frowning over Lyndsey's unscripted mood shift, had barely summed up the end of the scene, when Mr. Caparelli cut in with, "Okay, that's all we have time for today."

Everyone piled into the seats for notes. Mr. Beach and Ms. Lopez made their comments and then Mr. C. went over the acting, saving Lyndsey for last.

"Tell us again exactly why you want to change the script to portray Daffodil as angry instead of scared," he instructed her.

Lyndsey listed on her fingers:

"She puts up with this straw-to-gold nonsense for way too long, she doesn't tell the king off, she doesn't refuse to give up her firstborn child, she's a coward, I hate her."

"Valid reasons, I get your point," said Mr. C. "Here are mine: We're dealing with someone who's afraid for her life and really wants to end up a queen. As far as theater is concerned, if she becomes angry and stomps around the place, she's not enough contrast to Rumpelstiltskin. Samantha, anything to add?"

Samantha was eager to jump in. "I think she *has* to be scared. If she weren't scared, why would she agree to give up her baby? If she's brave enough to be angry, she would have figured out a way to escape."

"She'd never escape from us!" called out Michael and Neesha, risking checks by their names for this outburst.

"We should take a vote," said Lyndsey. "See what everyone thinks."

"Not going to happen," said Mr. Caparelli. "This is not a democracy, Ms. Ching. This is the theater."

We got up to leave. "Remember: *Learn. Your. Lines.*"

Mr. C. emphasized each word by pounding a partially rolled-up script on his palm.

—

BathRoom PRactice?

I saw Lyndsey violently wedging her script into her backpack. Daffodil might not get to be mad, but Lyndsey sure was. I approached the dangerous beast with caution. I haven't had a whole lot of practice talking to girls, much less angry Populars.

"Hey, Lyndsey, we've really *got* to practice together." She didn't reply. "Can we meet at your house yet?"

"Not yet," she said. "My parents are *still* painting it, you know? And I *still* can't have any guests. They're picky about people coming over when stuff isn't all perfect."

Not a promising start, but at least she wasn't looking around to see if her cool friends were watching.

"Well, you know *my* place is full of cat hair," I said. I thought for a moment. "What if we could find a spot in my house where my cat never goes?"

"*Is* there such a place?" asked Lyndsey. She made it sound like a dare.

"Well . . . of course the guaranteed best place would be somewhere like the refrigerator," I said. "But that's out."

"No kidding," said Lyndsey.

"So, the only place I can think of that's an actual

room is my parents' bathroom. Button never goes in there. They keep the door shut. Too bad for him. He'd like it—he loves licking water from the bottom of sinks." I was practically babbling, trying hard to get Lyndsey to lighten up.

Lyndsey cut in. "Are you seriously suggesting that we practice lines in a *bathroom?*"

"Have you got a better idea?"

"What about the guest room?"

"We don't have one," I said. "Well, we do, but it's my room. I sleep on the couch when my grandparents visit."

"The kitchen? The dining room? The garage?" Lyndsey was clearly steamed. "Geez, it's bad enough playing such a wimpy part. I am definitely not rehearsing it in a bathroom."

I racked my brain. "The garage might work. Of course it's so packed with junk there's not even room for a car."

We finally settled on meeting at my house Saturday morning at 10:00. With luck, Molly would be horseback riding until at least noon.

—

Bad Taste From Lunch

With the rehearsal over, my brain snapped back to the crappy mood I had been in earlier. I didn't feel like talking, but Kip was waiting for me outside. He'd stayed late in the computer lab and his mom was giving us a ride home.

"Got yourself a new girlfriend?" Kip nodded toward Lyndsey as she left.

"Oh, give me a break!" I snapped.

"Whoa—what's bugging *you?*"

"Nothing."

"Hey, that was convincing. Try again, Actor Man."

I sighed. "Okay, Bad Daniel moment at lunch."

"What happened? Where was I?"

"You'd already left. Daniel just showed up, mouthing off to some sixth graders about how he can tell who is gay and who isn't. Said I was clearly 'so gay' because I was in the musical and 'all guys in plays are fags.' I know it was just Daniel doing his little thing, but it still sucks to have to listen to it."

"There has *got* to be a way to get back at that Loser," said Kip fiercely.

"Even if there is," I said, "what if it backfires? Right now, he's keeping himself busy by tormenting everybody. No way I want to risk spending the rest of the year as his one special target."

—

Educating Molly

"Cut it out!" I yelled, as Molly thumped along on her fourth gallop—or was it a canter?—through the house, her ponytail bouncing wildly.

"Why? I'm not touching you!"

"I'm learning lines," I said. "And you're bugging me

with your dumb fake horse game. Besides, you'll freak out Button."

The memorizing wasn't going that well. I kept replaying my stupid brain's tape of what Daniel had said at lunch. I can handle stuff like that. Sort of.

"I'll do what I want, *Tofu*," Molly said, but she stopped, flopping down in front of me and making a face. She started scratching Button's back.

"You can't run around on all fours in middle school," I said, not looking up from my script.

"I don't do it at school *now*," she retorted. "Only at home. I'm not a moron, you know."

"Well, thank God," I said. I knew that was harsh, but I kept going. "Listen, there's a lot about middle school you better learn."

"Like what, Mr. Know It All?" Molly rolled over and yawned, then spent some time pulling out her elastic hair tie. But I knew she was paying attention.

I paused. "Well . . . you'll never be one of the popular kids if they find out you pretend to be a horse and jump over broomsticks or gallop around the house."

"Canter. And what do you mean I can't be popular when I get to middle school?" Molly looked incredulous, as if this were the last thing she'd expected me to say. "I have tons of friends now and we're all going to Hope Springs next year."

"Yeah, but when you get there, it won't be like fifth

grade. People get different. They'll start to like different stuff. And you won't fit in. Like for starters, you'd rather go to the ranch than the mall." Actually, I admired that about Molly, but I was on a roll.

"That's because no one ever *takes* me to the mall," objected Molly, snapping the hair tie across the room. "I'd like it a lot if I ever got to go."

"Come on, Magoo, you know what I mean," I said. "And another thing. You know kids who sort of rule the school and only hang out with each other, right? Don't even think about being one of them. Your best bet is to be a Medium—that's what Kip and I are."

"Oh, like I *really* want to be just like you and Kip," said Molly.

"Hey, listen, I'm serious. If you aren't careful, you'll get pegged as a Geek, or worse, a Loser."

"You're just trying to freak me out," said Molly. She stood up, glaring at me, fists on her hips.

"I am *not*," I said. "Ask anyone at my school."

"I don't *know* anyone at your school, except you and your annoying friends," said Molly. She leaped high over Button and did her horse thing out of the room.

It was pointless to even *try* with a sister.

I turned to the only one left in my audience. "You'd be a Medium, wouldn't you, Button?"

Button yawned, stretched, and curled one paw over his nose. I gently scratched his head. Button always lets me go on. He never interrupts.

"Not that I think you'd be happy in middle school," I added. "It isn't a good place for cats . . . or for actors."

CRUMB LiCKERS

"I think you're doing okay with Rumpelstiltskin's voice and all," said Kip. We were eating lunch at one of the beat-up picnic tables at the edge of the blacktop.

"How would you know?" asked Rusty, surprised.

"He's been helping me learn my lines," I explained. "Lyndsey's so hard to pin down, Kip's been coming over to read her part. Problem is, now he thinks he's some sort of expert on the play."

"Your problem," continued Kip, through a mouthful of apple, "is you're not looking short enough. The guy's supposed to be some sort of elf person. You gotta hunch over more or something. Heck, you're as tall as Rusty, and he's the king."

"Yeah, scrunch down before me, you little weirdo," put in Rusty.

"Well, *you* may be the right height for your part, Rusty," I grumbled, "but you sound too much . . . I don't know . . . like a smart-mouthed kid. Not like a king. You don't act like anyone who'd be able to talk someone into chopping off heads, much less do it yourself."

Rusty grabbed a shiny empty chips bag and jammed it on his head. Then he hopped up on the picnic table and pointed at Kip and me. "Bow down, you lowly serf types!" He ordered, in a fake deep voice.

Kids at other tables turned and stared.

"Bow down, and while you're there, clean up the crumbs from my royal table," continued Rusty.

"I don't think so, Kingie," said Kip, sticking his finger up his nose to show he meant it.

I made a fake bow and pretended to gag at the same time.

Rusty ignored us and went on louder. "Better yet, *lick* the crumbs up off my royal table. No, lick the ground *beneath* my royal table!"

Kip and I, embarrassed but laughing, jumped up on the bench and grabbed Rusty by the armpits and ankles. Then we hauled him off the table and stumbled across the blacktop, yelling, "Here comes the King! Look out for the crazy King!"

We plowed through a group shooting baskets and around a bench full of Goths, ending up in a heap on the grass. Students nearby laughed their heads off—some like they thought it was really funny, some like they were eager to prove we were not *their* friends.

I was laughing, too, trying to pretend I didn't see Daniel Brickster imitating us and laughing with his Loser friends. But inside, I wondered if it had been worth it.

Rehearsal at Cat-Hair House

It was raining hard Saturday morning. Of course Molly *would* pick this Saturday to not go to the ranch. I had begged my parents to take her somewhere—*anywhere*—but they refused to see there was a problem.

I made some space in the garage, and tried to set things up for rehearsing. My plan was to run outside when I heard Lyndsey's car, take her directly into the garage, and avoid the house and Molly completely. But the doorbell rang at 9:52. She was early. So much for my plan.

Molly raced to the door.

"Beat it, okay?" I said. "It's for me."

"Is it your girlfriend?" asked Molly, with a big smile, her hand on the knob.

"No!" I barked. "I don't have a girlfriend. Now get lost!"

"Not until I meet her," said Molly, opening the door.

"Hi," I said to Lyndsey, pushing Molly aside. "Come on in."

"I'm Molly," said Molly. "Do you ride?"

"My dad drove me because of the rain," said Lyndsey, looking confused.

"She means ride horses, and you don't have to talk to her," I said.

"Maybe she wants to," said Molly. She smiled at Lyndsey. "My lesson was canceled, so I'm not riding today. Are you in Topher's play? You have really pretty hair. I wish my hair was straight like that."

"Um, thanks," said Lyndsey. "We're going to practice

here today. We just have to find a place with no cat hair, you know? I'm allergic."

"Ew, what happens? Do you throw up or stop breathing?" Molly asked.

"Molly, beat it!" I gave her a shove. She stepped back but didn't leave. I turned to Lyndsey. "I've made a space for us in the garage. It's not heated, but at least it doesn't have cat hair."

"Okay, let's try it," said Lyndsey.

"This way," I said. "Molly, get lost, or I'm telling Dad. I mean it."

"Like I'm real worried, *Tofu*," she said. But she headed toward her room. "Button's in here, Lyndsey," she called over her shoulder. "In case you stop being allergic and want to see him." Then she closed the door.

I hurried us to the garage, in case Molly came out again. We sat on two of the three big boxes I'd arranged near the only window. I squeezed around the car to get to them, and, in my hurry, tipped over a huge bag full of Styrofoam pellets. They billowed around the garage.

"It's just like snow!" I said, immediately wishing I had not—full-on dork moment. But Lyndsey smiled. "I was thinking it was kind of cold in here, you know?"

"Need a blanket? Hot chocolate?" I held up an old quilt and the thermos I'd brought out earlier.

This time she really laughed. "You thought of everything!"

"Let's hope I can think of my lines," I said.

It seemed too embarrassing to sing with just the two of us there, and we decided to skip that and just speak the words when we got to a song. But after a while, we realized it was easier to remember the lyrics with music playing. I switched on the CD player, balanced on box number three, and before long, we were belting out the ridiculous tunes and feeling warmer.

—

Bossy Little In-charge Show-off

"I've never liked 'Ring Around the Rosie,'" I said as Kip, Rusty, and I collected stuff from our lockers after school. "And now I have to sing it in front of everyone, only to Samantha's words."

"Hey, we could ask Mr. C. if he'd think about changing the music to better tunes," said Rusty. "Of course, Ms. Lopez would have a fit, but she'd get over it."

"I doubt that," I said. "But I was thinking of asking Samantha to pick another tune for 'She'll Never Guess It.'"

"There's no music in *your* play, right, Kip?" said Rusty. "I bet if enough people ask, Mr. C. would figure out a way to put it on, too. We've still got a month. And a lot of the teachers would be all for it. We could start a petition. It would be a cinch to get a lot of signatures."

"Excellent idea!" I said. "Hey, remember when they gave out two Olympic gold medals for the same skating thing? So we should be able to have two winning plays."

But Kip held up his hands to stop us. "Don't do it, okay?" he said. "I mean, it's cool of you guys to like it that much, but even if it could happen, I don't want to do it, at least not right now."

I stared at him. "What do you mean? You wanted to win, I know you did. You were really bummed when you didn't."

Kip shook his head. "First of all, there's no way the school will agree to do two plays at once. And second, I just couldn't handle doing my play right now—all the comments and people wanting changes and stuff. I mean, what if everybody decided I was making fun of blind people by having Little Candy Apple pretend not to be able to see? Or what if some kids kept bugging me to take out lines I really like? I don't know how Samantha puts up with it."

"Okay," I said. "Whatever you want. But I think it's a real waste for people not to get to see your play, too."

"Is Samantha like your girlfriend or something?" asked Rusty, looking at Kip with suspicion.

Kip rolled his eyes. "Oh, right. Me and the Geek Princess."

He left to catch the bus, and Rusty and I headed for rehearsal.

I kept thinking about what Kip had said about Samantha. Could such a bossy little in-charge show-off really be having a tough time?

At the break, I hung around outside with Rusty and José. After a while, I bought a root beer from the machine and walked over to Samantha, sitting by herself on the hall floor outside the auditorium. She was staring at the script, chewing on a pencil and twirling a strand of hair on her finger. She must have been at this for a while, judging from the collection of hair knots all over her head. They looked pretty funny, but I had a feeling she didn't want to hear that. She looked up when I sat down next to her, but didn't say anything. She went back to writing something on the script and twisting her hair.

I opened my can of soda. "Rehearsals are going pretty good now, don't you think? Seems like we're finally not making a mess of your play."

Samantha shrugged, but said nothing.

I tried again. "Do you like that bit José does, where the Miller's bragging to the Guards and puffs out his chest so much he falls over backward? I bet the audience will love it."

Samantha sighed. "Topher, you know kids are making fun of this play every chance they get. It doesn't matter that it's *supposed* to be funny, or that everyone is starting to do a good job." She gave the strand of hair she was twisting a yank. "The kids who've decided it's for babies are telling that to everyone else, so I don't know if *anyone* besides people's moms will come to the shows."

"Who'd you hear that from?" I asked. "Daniel Brickster? Brittani Aren't-I-Cool?" I pulled the ring off the root beer can with a jerk. "Come on, lots of kids will come, especially after they hear how funny it is."

"I *wish*," said Samantha. "Anyway, I thought if I could rewrite some of the lines to be even funnier, it would help. Or maybe I really should try making Daffodil tougher."

"Are you nuts?" I said. "You can't write just to please certain people. Next thing you know, people will want you to change lines they don't like." (Or music, I thought, with a touch of guilt.) "Look, just forget it. I'll bet you anything this play will not be a flop." I was wishing I really believed that.

I flicked the ring from the soda can against the opposite wall. It hit with a tiny clink.

—

Cold Chocolate Fear

"Mom?" I called. "Where are you? Can you take us to the movie now?"

It was Saturday afternoon. All week, Kip and I had been looking forward to seeing *Cold Chocolate Fear*, a movie about humanoid aliens landing near a shopping mall and getting jobs at the Dairy Queen. The ads on TV made it look scary, funny, and gross—a winning combination.

I found my mom in the laundry room, kneeling by the basket where Button slept at night. "I think he's getting worse," she said, ignoring what I'd said about the movie. I looked down at Button. He was stretched out on a pile of green blanket. I thought my cat was looking more and more like a plush toy with the stuffing taken out.

"He's not eating," said Mom. "And he's not even drinking water like he has been."

"Maybe he's finally had enough food and water for a while," I said hopefully. "I mean, maybe he's actually starting to get better."

She looked up at me and smiled. "Wouldn't that be great?" But she didn't look excited.

I read the clock on the dryer. The movie was starting in twenty minutes. "Are you going to take him to Dr. Casey's now?" I asked.

"I think I better," said Mom. "Would you and Kip put him in his carrier while I get my purse?" She hurried to her bedroom.

"Maybe she'll take us first," I said, as Kip walked into the laundry room. "I don't know why she's worried," I added. "I mean, I don't think Button looks worse, do you?"

Kip just shrugged and held the lid open while I put Button in the cardboard cat carrier. Button meowed with annoyance, but didn't struggle to get out the way he would have a year ago. As usual, however, he started yowling the moment the lid was fastened, and that made me feel oddly relieved.

Button hated the carrier, he hated riding in the car, he hated being in the vet's office, he hated any and all cats that were in the waiting room, and he hated the shiny metal table Dr. Casey put him on to examine him. At least he didn't seem to mind Dr. Casey. When the ordeal was over and Button was home, he would spend forever cleaning himself all over, like he was trying to lick the whole experience off his body.

As Mom started the car, I tried asking about the movie again. "Are you taking us first?" I said, trying to sound like it didn't matter.

"Taking you where?" she asked, sounding distracted, as she backed out of the driveway.

"The movie, remember? It starts in, like, ten minutes," I reminded her.

"You know this is your cat, too, Topher," she said, her voice getting that tight sound.

"I know, I know, it's fine, it doesn't matter. It's just, you know, on the way and all." I slumped in my seat, holding the cat carrier on my lap.

I could see this was a lose/lose situation—I'd feel guilty if we went to the movie and sorry for myself and for Kip if we didn't. Mom pulled up right in front of the movie theater.

"Have you got money for this with you?"

"Yeah, we both do," I said. "Look, Mom, we can go another time, really."

She handed me a couple bucks. "You boys will need this for the bus home." She smiled a C-minus smile. "Have fun." And she drove off, Button yowling.

We bought our tickets and headed for the door showing *Cold Chocolate Fear*.

I was probably scowling because Kip said, "Are you okay?"

"Me? Sure!" I said, with bitter cheerfulness. "Why wouldn't I be okay? I'm off to see a movie instead of standing beside my poor sick cat, holding his paw in his hour of need. Too bad I don't have enough money to get popcorn so I can have something to choke on and die to serve me right for being so heartless."

"Oh, cut it out," said Kip.

—

Straw Into Gold

Lyndsey/Daffodil put her head in her hands and pretended to sob.

That was my cue. I scrunched myself down and tried to both march and waddle onto the stage, shouting—above the sobbing—"Stop that crying!" I could hear giggling. By the time I finished my song, the rest of the cast was really laughing. I felt a rush of excitement, like soda bubbles racing through my body. I let myself really cut loose, waving my arms and pretending to pull at my (still imaginary) fake beard as I sang.

I spun the bike wheel and the lights went down—or

would when the tech crew was in place—and slowly, one by one, Straw pieces took off their outer costumes— yellow baggy pajamas and floppy hats covered with glued-on straw. When they stood up, they revealed the gold costumes underneath—shiny gold-colored bike shorts and long-sleeved gold-colored tees, topped by shiny gold-painted swim caps.

When the lights came back up, the Straw—now Gold—was standing in a circle. Each piece of Gold had his or her arms raised, palms together, and was leaning toward the others, forming a sort of shiny tent of kids. The music started in on their happy song, "We Were Straw, But Now We're Gold," and they joined hands in the center of the tent-shape, skipping in a circle and waving their outside arms in the air to the music.

I hardly paid attention during notes, which were mostly for the Straw. In my head, I kept replaying the scene and rehearing the laughter. The *good* kind of laughter— the kind I wanted to hear forever.

—

Horse Show

"But I *have* to be in eight events," Molly was saying to Mom when I came down for breakfast, a few days later. "This is the first show of the year! Pleeease?"

"I didn't say you couldn't *be* in eight events," said Mom. "I said I won't *pay* for eight. I'll pay for four. You'll have to cover the rest."

"But that's so unfair!" wailed Molly. "I'll never have enough money."

"Well, we have that in common," said our mother, flashing her fake smile. Molly scowled in return, furiously buttering her toast.

"Are you riding Mr. Muffin Man in the show?" I asked, flooding my Cheerios with milk. I wanted to get Molly onto a happier part of the topic.

"I hope so," she said, through a mouthful of raisin toast. "If his leg is okay by then. He's been a little lame all week, so nobody's ridden him much. If I don't get to ride Mr. Muffin Man, I'm stuck with Piewacket and who knows *what* she'll be like."

She went on about the various horses at the ranch where she rode, and I nodded as she talked, but I wasn't really paying attention. My mind was on the rehearsal after school.

Yesterday, the Straw kept forgetting their dance steps, and Rusty kept losing his place and having to start over, and I could *not* get the tune right to the song where Rumpelstiltskin sings about his name and the King overhears. Mr. Caparelli had to break up a shoving match between three members of the Straw. And Neesha had refused to join hands with Michael in an earlier scene when they were blocking Daffodil's exit, because his fingers were sticky from Skittles. But otherwise things had gone pretty well.

REHEARSAL #26—THE BEARD EFFECT

At the next rehearsal, everyone else was handed their props and the parts to their costumes. I checked the hanger with my costume pieces on it:

Hat? Check.

Beard? Check.

Tunic? Check.

There was a note pinned to the tunic, reminding me I had to provide my own black shoes—preferably soft ones—a long-sleeved black T-shirt or turtleneck, and black tights.

The hat was red and made of some soft material. It had a tall peak that flopped over to one side. The tunic was a raggedy patchwork number, sleeveless and coming down to just above my knees.

But best of all was the long, gray fake beard. It had elastic loops that hooked on over my ears. The rest of the costume was good, but the beard made all the difference. Even though Mr. Stickle didn't have even a mustache, much less a long, gray beard, wearing this fake one put me most definitely in a Mr. Stickle space, a cranky-little-man space. I slipped it on over my ears, went onstage, and felt like I really *was* Rumpelstiltskin.

I had an inspiration. I turned my head to one side and spat, just like I'd seen Mr. Stickle do. Then immediately I had an even better idea. Pinching my nose with my fingers, I leaned over and blew a fine spray of snot onto the floor. There was a gasp from Lyndsey, who jumped back, looking grossed out. Kids howled with laughter, then turned to see how Mr. Caparelli was taking it.

Mr. C. seemed to be having a fit, either from laughing or coughing or both—it was hard to tell. Finally, he recovered. "Topher, you can clean this up and never pull a stunt like that again, or it's a fifth check by your name, and you know what that will mean."

"I was just getting into the character," I defended myself. "This fairy tale takes place a really long time ago, and we learned in history class that's how they blew their noses before there were handkerchiefs or tissues."

Apparently this may have been an *explanation*, but not—as my dad would put it—an excuse. I promised never to do it again, and headed for the boys' room to get paper towels.

My mind was a jumble of thoughts—the rush of the laughter. And did I really have four checks? Already? I *never* got stuff like checks. It felt great. I was almost tempted to go for it. But the sight of my costumed self in the bathroom mirror stopped me. I loved being Rumpelstiltskin. There was no way I'd risk being kicked out of the play.

—

HYPOCRITE

Dress rehearsal was next Thursday, six days away. How could it be so soon? Even counting that last rehearsal, we had only four rehearsals left.

"I want everybody here for each of the remaining rehearsals at 4:00 P.M. sharp," said Mr. C. Then looking right at me, he added, "I want you *all* here with the right attitude, and no smart-alecky stage business. Is that clear?"

Waiting for the bus with Rusty, I barely noticed his usual motormouth.

Mr. C. was being a hypocrite. First he said to model the character after someone; then he got all Miss Manners when I showed a little creativity. "The man has no imagination," I said out loud, totally confusing Rusty, who had been talking about a new X-Men game.

—

MR. CLUELESS AND MISS BOSSY BUTT

"Dad, can you give me a ride to the school?" I asked. "I gotta help with the sets." It was Saturday morning and I'd overslept. Now I was shoveling down my breakfast.

"I'll do better than give you a ride," said my dad. "I'm going over to work on the sets myself."

I had to take an extra big slug of milk to cover my annoyance. I knew I should be glad he was helping. All the parents were *supposed* to volunteer for some part of the work on the show, but a lot of them never did squat. All the same, it always makes me tense whenever my dad or mom is at school. You never know when they'll bust out with something embarrassing.

I swallowed the milk. "Is that what you're wearing?" I

asked, trying to sound casual, as I eyed his sweatshirt. It was dark blue, torn, and paint-splattered, which was fine. But it had "My Dad Rocks!" on it in bright yellow letters—a gift from Molly several Christmases ago.

"Yeah, I love this sweatshirt. I'm going to be sorry to see it go." Clueless once again. I sighed and took my plate to the sink.

We loaded some rags and newspapers and a painters' tarp into the car and took off.

"Dad, today while you're there? Just don't say anything in your Weirdo voice, okay?"

"You mean *dees vone?*" Dad was grinning and talking in the fake German (or was it Russian?) accent he loved to use when answering the phone. "Or—do—you—mean—this—one?" Now he was sounding like a TV alien.

"Yeah! Don't do it!" I was already sorry I'd brought it up, now that we were on our way. Obviously, all I'd done was give the guy ideas.

"I'll try to behave myself," said my dad, chuckling. We drove the rest of the way in silence. We were just walking into the theater, when he said, "But it's okay if I sing, right?"

"Not funny, Dad."

This was the major Saturday set-painting day, and there were several parents and a few kids already hard at work. Ray, a college guy who was in charge of set design and construction, got me started on some background bushes, and Dad went off to work on Daffodil's dungeon walls.

Samantha, who had come with her mom, was already working on the bushes. Seemed like lately she was acting less geeky. Today she was actually dressed like a normal kid, except for this purple-flowered scarf she had tied around her head. I guess it was to keep her hair from getting in the paint, but it looked really dumb.

I said hi, picked up a brush, and dipped it in a big bucket of green paint.

"It's all getting pretty close now, huh?" said Samantha.

I nodded and started painting.

Samantha put down her brush. She seemed up to something. "Listen, I don't want you to take this the wrong way," she said, voice low. "I mean, you're doing a good job as Rumpelstiltskin. . . ."

"But?"

She smiled apologetically. "Yeah, well, *but,* I don't think you're scary enough. I mean, you're way funny and all, but I always pictured Rumpelstiltskin as this sinister old magician. You're not sinister or magical."

"Sorry."

"No, I mean that's good in real life, but I wish you could be more that way in the show."

"Mr. C. talked to me a lot about how to act this part. *He* seems okay with what I'm doing. And *he's* the director."

"And I only wrote the play, is that what you mean? I

don't get to have any say in how it's done?" Samantha's voice was rising.

"Maybe you don't!" I was getting really steamed. Why was she so bossy?

"So you think being grouchy and bouncy is all you have to do? Just lurch around onstage and everyone will really believe you're someone who knows real magic?"

"What's this got to do with real magic?"

"How do you think he turns the straw to gold? Just by yelling at it?"

This remark was over the top, and I was this close to painting her face green. Then I noticed people were staring. My dad, for one. My face got very hot.

"You're a real bossy butt," I said at last, under my breath. I went back to painting.

—

Parent Trap

"Why so quiet?" asked Mom later that afternoon. I was helping her do yard work—mostly raking leaves.

"Nothing, I guess. I just don't like people who aren't directors telling me how to be an actor."

"What people?"

I jabbed the rake into the leaf pile I had made. "Samantha," I said. "The World's Most Wonderful Scriptwriter, remember?"

Mom started loading leaves into a plastic bag. "Is she trying to tell you how to act?" she asked.

"Oh, she's so annoying. She claims I'm not making

Rumpelstiltskin *magical* enough. That I'm just making him funny and grouchy, and that's not enough. Or something like that. She wants him to do the magic stuff—you know, straw into gold—in a *believable* way. It's a *fairy tale*. What does it matter how it's done? It's all make-believe anyway."

"Hmm. Well, I see why that would tick you off." Mom sat down on the leaf bag. "Now don't get me wrong, I agree this is a matter for Mr. Caparelli, not Samantha, but I think I know what she means."

"Oh, thanks for taking *my* side," I said, thumping the rake onto the ground.

"Hang on," said Mom, "it's not a taking-sides thing. When I was a volunteer at the rehearsal the other day, I thought you were very funny. And I told you so, remember? But you weren't *magical*. Wait! Listen to me on this, okay?"

I had started to walk off, but now I flopped down in the leaves—trapped in another Parental Advice Moment. Nothing to do but wait it out.

Mom said, "Of course it's just make-believe, but not to the character. In the story, Rumpelstiltskin's really doing it. You need to have some idea in your head *how*. Maybe you could make up some secret incantation, some magic he learned from a sorceress a hundred years ago."

"We're not allowed to add stuff to our lines."

"Not your lines, your head—to how you're thinking while you're onstage."

She got up and started re-raking the leaves. After a moment, I did, too. As much as I hated having my own mother side with Miss Bossy Butt, I thought about what Samantha meant. About believing in the magic as long as I was Rumpelstiltskin. Not that I would, but if for some reason all my own I decided to, how exactly could I do that?

—

Is That Legal?

I was just getting started on the Sunday comics when Mom came into the living room, looking for trouble.

"Don't you need to do all your homework now, if you have rehearsals every day this week?" She was giving me The Look.

"*Mom,* it's under control."

She rolled her eyes and left.

I was tempted to go on reading, but she'd no doubt be back to check on me. She had obviously forgotten what it was like to be forced to do homework before reading the funnies. Sunday comics probably didn't even *exist* when she was a kid. Or there were only two and they were black-and-white.

With final dress rehearsal on Thursday, and opening night Friday, I really did need to catch up on school-work. I got my backpack and pulled out my math book and binder. I had a feeling there was something I was supposed to do besides homework—but what?

I found Button in a sun spot under the table and carried him to the couch. Button always disliked being placed somewhere, no matter how warm and cozy it was, and would usually jump right up and go off to sit and lick himself in a resentful way. But this time he stayed, curled up next to me, his head and one paw on the homework handout sheet.

The vet had kept him overnight so they could decide about changing how much insulin he got every day. He seemed to be eating and drinking more since he got back home, but I still missed the old race-around-the-house Button.

The doorbell rang. "Can somebody get that?" I called. I waited a minute, but no one came. I sighed and got up cautiously, trying, out of habit, to keep Button from leaping off the couch. I was almost sad when he stayed—another reminder of his illness.

Robbie Newsome was at the door. "My mom says she has to give these back to you. She says she forgot we have to go to Grandma's this weekend." He was holding out four tickets.

Tickets! That was it. I had completely spaced on selling the rest of my tickets. And now they were coming back. Was that legal?

Robbie headed for my bedroom. I pulled him back.

"Can't she just give them to someone else?"

"I don't know," said Robbie. "I'll ask."

He came back a minute later, this time with Banana leaping at his heels. Across the street, Mrs. Newsome was calling to the dog. "She says she doesn't know any-one who would go, so she needs her money back," said Robbie.

I groaned. I searched the hall table for the ticket enve-lope. I found it under the two big award ribbons Molly had won the day before in her horse show. Inside the envelope were the remaining tickets and two measly checks. I handed Mrs. Newsome's to Robbie, managing to keep Banana from bounding into the house and scar-ing another year off Button's life.

"Here," I said. "Have fun at your grandma's."

"I will," said Robbie. "She has a pool."

After he left, I dumped out the envelope and surveyed the pitiful pile. There was the check from my mom for five tickets. My parents were going twice and had bought one for Molly. There was also some cash to cover two tickets, bought by two of Molly's friends who were going with her. That made seven tickets sold. Ten minutes ago, it had been eleven. That meant I now had to sell thirteen, not nine. (Math—useful in everyday life, just like the teachers promised.) Obviously I had to try to sell these today, since it was the last weekend before the play. I put the envelope back on the table and went to get dressed.

I heard the front door slam as I was getting on my shoes. Molly must have come back from riding. That made twice this weekend. She'd go every day if she could. I could hear voices and the thumps of boots com-ing off. Her friend Nicole was probably with her. I was not in the mood for fifth-grade girls. I popped a CD into my portable player and flopped down on my bed. I told myself I would just lie down for a minute, to psyche myself up for door-to-door sales. Okay, maybe ten minutes. I closed my eyes.

I woke up when Dad came into the room with a pile of clean laundry.

"Hey, Topher, I thought you were doing homework, buddy."

"Just resting my eyes. I'll do it now." I said and staggered blearily to my feet.

"Put these away first," he said, and headed back to the laundry room.

I scooped up the clothes and shoved them into my top two drawers. I looked at my watch. I must have been asleep for almost an hour. Rats! I still hadn't done any homework, and Kip was coming over in thirty minutes to help me rehearse. Well, I'd use that time to try to sell tickets.

I went back to the hall table. Molly's horse show ribbons were still there, but my large envelope was nowhere to be seen.

—

The Lucky Cyclist

"Where's my big envelope with the tickets in it?" I shouted to no one in particular. Geez, I hardly had any stupid time left, and now the stupid envelope was missing. I checked the hall table again, tossing aside magazines, old mail, and a report Molly had gotten an A on two weeks before, which she kept replacing conspicuously on top of the pile.

"Right where you left it, on the hall table," my dad called back from the laundry room. He walked in, carrying a stack of folded towels. "Is it missing? I told you not to leave it so near the front door."

"It was here earlier, I swear." This could not be happening. I looked on the floor, then checked the furniture, lifting cushions and flopping them back down, fuming the whole time.

When Kip arrived, I still hadn't found the tickets. I pictured every performance of the play with the cast facing empty seats that were all my fault.

Kip walked in, holding out a half-full paper cup. "Want some?" he asked.

"What's in there?" I asked, eyeing pink liquid in the cup.

"It was sold to me as lemonade—geez, do you think it's spiked?" Kip held it at arm's length in mock horror. "I bought it from a suspicious pair of fifth graders on the corner." Then he shrugged and gulped it down.

"Oh, don't tell me Molly's still doing the lemonade stand," I said. "It's practically December."

"Yeah, plus she's got a side business going in ticket orders. I bought one from her for the Sunday matinee—figured I might as well go twice."

"What? Where'd she get . . ." I suddenly figured it out.

"The little snot rag! She took my envelope!" I started out the door. Kip grabbed my arm, but I kept striding down the sidewalk.

"Where are you going?" demanded Kip, letting go, but trotting along beside me.

"To get my envelope back, that's where!"

"Go for it, Rumpelstiltskin," said Kip.

"What do you mean?" I snapped, but Kip only rolled his eyes.

Rounding the corner, we spotted Molly and Nicole at the end of the block. The girls had set up a small table and two chairs, with an umbrella strapped to one of the chairs. I could see a pitcher, cups, and a cooler. Molly was handing something through the window of a car that had pulled up to the curb.

I slowed down. I didn't want to look too weird to the people in the car by actually running up there, but I was seething. The car pulled away as Molly and Nicole waved and called, "Thank you!" I ran up to them.

"What's the big idea, Molly?" I hadn't meant to sneak up on them, but Nicole jumped a mile and Molly turned to me in surprise, her big grin and wave dissolving.

"That's mine! Hand it over." I grabbed the envelope from Nicole, who had been putting something in it.

"Just grab it out of her hands, why don't you, jerk-weed!" said Molly, recovering from her surprise and now looking hurt, as well as angry. "We were doing you a favor, since you hadn't sold any tickets for a month, but forget it." She turned and ripped down a sign I had seen only from the back. It said,

BUY A TICKET, GET A FREE WINTER LEMONADE!!!
REGULAR PRICE 50¢

I looked in the envelope. I tried to stay mad, but the sight of the contents stopped me. The envelope was stuffed with dollar bills and checks and there was only one ticket left.

"Oh, wow," was all I could think of to say. "Oh, wow." I looked up. Molly, Kip, and Nicole were all staring at me in silence. "This is amazing."

Molly looked away, giving a small shrug. "Well, don't worry, *Tofu*, I won't do it again." She was blinking a lot.

I let out a big breath. "Um, okay, I'm sorry I got so mad, Magoo."

She glared at me and folded her arms viciously. "You didn't have to totally freak out like that. I thought you'd be all happy I'd done you this huge favor. I was going to surprise you."

"Oh, I'm surprised all right. Look, I said I'm sorry. It's just that you had me really worried about losing the tickets and money and Mom's check and all. So if you want to, you know, sell this last ticket . . ." My voice trailed off.

"Actually, I don't feel like it anymore," said Molly.

At the far end of the street, a bike rider, in full racing Lycra, was pedaling toward us.

"Come on, let's get him!" said Nicole.

Molly hesitated, then apparently couldn't help herself. It just wasn't in her to let a potential customer slip by. She leaped up, waving her arms. Nicole did the same. They hopped on and off the curb, doing a little dance and shouting, "*Lemonade! World's Best Lemonade!*"

The cyclist pulled to a stop.

"You are so lucky!" said Molly giving him her best grin. "We have a special, today only. If you buy a ticket to the Hope Springs Middle School musical, you can have a *free* winter lemonade. That saves you fifty cents!"

The cyclist smiled. "Well, actually I don't—"

"*This* is the star!" interrupted Molly. She gestured grandly toward me. "He's my brother! He's tall to be Rumpelstiltskin, but he's great." As if that explained away any hesitations the man might have. (Of course, now I was feeling like the major meanie of the world.)

"Oh, well, why not?" said the cyclist, unzipping a tiny pouch by his waist. "How much for the ticket?"

"Ten dollars is all," said Molly. The guy hesitated, but Nicole quickly handed him the ticket and Molly gave him a brimming paper cup of lemonade. "That's for the Saturday night show at 8:00. And guess what? You just bought our last ticket! Talk about lucky!"

"Lucky indeed." He smiled again. "Say, what makes it a 'winter lemonade'?"

"No ice!" said Molly and Nicole together.

The cyclist drank the lemonade in one long gulp, zipped the ticket into his little pouch, and took off.

I shook my head in amazement. "You're so good at that, Molly, it's scary. I could have said all the same words and the guy probably would have left without even buying a drink."

Molly looked pleased.

—

Monday: A Crazy Idea

We were working on the beginning of Act II, and it had *not* been a great rehearsal. Since Act II didn't have any Straw or Gold in it, those kids were given various new parts to play—mostly scenery. But they kept forgetting where to stand, acting like dopes, falling over, whispering jokes.

Suddenly Lyndsey burst into tears. "This is totally stupid!" she screamed. "I hate this dumb play. I keep trying to do this right and everyone keeps acting stupid and messing it up. Daffodil is such a wimp, she *deserves* to have her head chopped off. I quit!"

Then, as we all watched in astonishment, she pulled off the long, curly blond wig, threw it and her script on the floor, and stomped out of the auditorium.

"Now see here, Lyndsey . . ." Mr. Caparelli started toward the door, but Ms. Lopez had already jumped up from the piano and was hurrying out after Lyndsey. We all watched as first Lyndsey and then Ms. Lopez raced out of the theater. I saw Kip step aside as they rushed past. He'd been sitting out in the hall doing homework, waiting to get a ride home with me, and had probably looked in to see what the shouting was about.

"I *knew* we needed understudies," muttered Mr. Caparelli. He breathed out a long *whoosh* of air. "So. We need a Daffodil for the rest of this rehearsal. Anyone know her lines?"

This was met by silence.

"Well, looks like I'll have to read them," said Mr. C.

We started back in where Rumpelstiltskin says, "What do I need with riches? Give me the baby. I kept my promise. Now you must keep yours."

"*No. No. That I cannot do,*" read Mr. C., sounding like a robot Daffodil and making no attempt to cry. Unfortunately, he did take a stab at the duet, "Hand Over the Babe." It was pretty dreadful. He knew about three notes and he just used them over and over. It was all I could do to remember the tune. We got through that finally, but then Mr. C. had to switch from Daffodil to director and tell the Straw-turned-garden not to move around like a storm was coming.

Ms. Lopez returned, her sugar smile looking a lot less sweet. No Lyndsey.

Mr. Caparelli was trying to find his place in the script, but finally breathed out another of those long whooshes of air. "Anybody want to read these lines instead of me? Of course, I realize no one has them memorized."

That's not exactly true, I thought. And right then, I was hit with an idea so crazy, it almost knocked me down. My hand went up before I could stop it.

"Mr. C.? I know someone who already knows most of Daffodil's lines," I said.

Mr. C. stared at me.

"Who?" he asked.

"Okay, remember when we were all talking about how in Shakespeare's time even the girls' parts were played by guys?"

Mr. Caparelli crossed his arms and nodded. I went on in a rush. "Well, wouldn't it be really funny if a boy had that wig on and was Daffodil?"

"*What?*" said everyone all at once.

Mr. C. shushed them. "Are you saying you know a boy who knows Daffodil's lines?" he demanded.

"Well, he knows most of them," I said. "He only learned them to help me practice."

Apparently I wasn't the only one who had noticed Kip when Lyndsey rushed past him. Now all the kids and Mr. C. looked toward the back of the theater. Kip's face was beet red, but he didn't disappear into the hall. I knew this had to work or I would be short one best friend.

"We can show you the scene right now," I said. I picked up the wig. I put it on my head. I was still wearing the long gray beard. I squeaked a couple of lines from Daffodil's first song: *"It isn't fair, it can't be true, I'm told to spin what none can do!"*

Several of the kids giggled and snorted. Samantha was not one of them.

"Mr. Caparelli, this is not the way my play is supposed to be done." Samantha stepped quickly to center stage.

"I know, I know," said Mr. C. "But hang on, Samantha, this is just for this rehearsal, until Lyndsey comes back. And it's giving me some new ideas." He rubbed his palms together, smiling for the first time all day. "Let's see what they can do."

I took off the wig and held it up to Kip. "Just this once?" I asked. There was a long pause, then Kip shrugged and, still red-faced, walked onto the stage and took the wig. He put it on his head. It had fit nicely on Lyndsey, but Kip's buzz cut and slightly smaller head made the fit less than perfect. The bangs hung way down into his eyes. He just stood there for a moment.

Then, magically, the wig seemed to get him in a Daffodil sort of mood. He walked over to the chair that was Daffodil's throne and sat down like he was adjusting a long skirt, just the way Lyndsey had done it. There were giggles of appreciation for this move. I started from my entrance, hunkering down and pulling on the beard as I approached the throne.

"*Good day, lovely queen,*" I said. This line had never gotten a laugh with Lyndsey as Daffodil. But this was a whole new Daffodil. Everyone cracked up. But nothing like they did after Kip's first line.

Kip opened his eyes and mouth wide in exaggerated surprise. "*Oh, good day, Little Man! I haven't any straw for you to spin to gold. In fact, gold-wise, I am pretty well set.*"

"*I didn't come to work,*" I said. "*I came to collect my payment. Remember our bargain?*" I reached out my hands for the "baby," currently someone's wadded-up sweatshirt.

Kip jumped up, clutching the sweatshirt wad to his skinny chest. "*Wait! You can't be serious! Here, take any treasure you see—want these rings? This throne? How about my crown?*"

"*No way!*" I said, hardly able to make myself heard over the laughing. "*What do I need with riches? Hand over the babe. I kept my promise. Now you must keep yours.*" I reached out for the sweatshirt-wad baby.

Kip did a great Daffodil, bursting into tears, then started our duet of "Hand Over the Babe."

When the scene was over, the rest of the cast burst into applause—all except Samantha.

It was 6:00 P.M., and Mr. C. dismissed us without notes this time. Samantha furiously gathered up the sheets of the script that Lyndsey had flung on the floor earlier.

Mr. Caparelli came over to Kip and me.

"So, what'd you think?" I asked.

"Pretty funny, I gotta say." Mr. C. was smiling. "You

really do know those lines, Kip." He rubbed his hands together again. "You boys are onto something. This scene was ten times funnier with a boy in the Daffodil part. What do you think?" He said this to Samantha, who had joined us, clutching the rejected script.

"First of all, I don't care how much Lyndsey doesn't agree with how I write, actors don't get to change lines they don't like," Samantha stated, like it was a traffic law. "Second, this is a part for a girl, not a boy. I want it to be a funny play, but not like *this*." She gestured toward Kip like he was some hopeless science project. "And third, isn't there a rule that cast members can't quit?"

"Hey, calm down. I bet she'll be back tomorrow," said Mr. C., avoiding a direct answer. "But, if for some crazy reason she *doesn't* change her mind, I really think we should seriously consider using Kip. I think we can exaggerate the humor in a lot of other scenes, like where—"

"Excuse me, Mr. Caparelli, but don't I get to say something here?" Kip was almost sputtering. "I never said I'd do it more than this once. Do you have any idea how much razzing I'll get when people find out I did even this *one* scene? No way will I do the whole play!"

"Okay, okay." Mr. C. held up his hands. "Nobody's making you do anything. Lyndsey probably just needs a night to cool off. Still, you and Topher really showed us how to push the fun in this play." He looked encouragingly at Samantha. But she had been waiting for him to agree with her and was clearly ticked that he wasn't going to. She didn't say anything more, and Kip and I left to wait for my mom to give us a ride.

As we stepped outside, we saw Lyndsey walking quickly away from the door. "Hey, Lyndsey," I called. She kept walking.

That ticked me off. This time I yelled, "We know you were watching the scene!"

Lyndsey climbed into an SUV that had just pulled up.

"Maybe she's getting kidnapped," said Kip, sounding almost hopeful.

—

TUESDAY: WORD IS OUT

By the next day, everyone had heard about Lyndsey quitting the play. They had also heard about Kip filling in. Even kids who didn't give a rat's zit about the play and weren't planning to go—at least not until now—were talking about it.

"Yo, T-Man, where's that faggy pal of yours, little Kippy?" Daniel said to me from his too-close locker. I usually try not to be there when he is, but this time I barely registered the insult. I had just seen Lyndsey walking down the hall. For once, she was alone. I slammed my locker shut and ran to catch up with her.

"What is *wrong* with you?" I demanded. "Did you really quit?"

"Yeah, I really quit!" Lyndsey shot back. "I hate the way Samantha didn't give Daffodil a brain in her head. I hate how Daffodil is such a mental lightweight she has to cheat to learn Rumpelstiltskin's name." She was giving me this up-yours look, scarcely pausing for breath. "And then Kip shows up *really* treating my part like a big joke."

"What do you mean 'your part'? You quit, remember?" I was feeling even less sorry for her than I was the day before. "Anyway, the whole *play* is a big joke."

Lyndsey started to walk away, but I remembered what I really wanted to ask her. "Hey, and by the way, why'd you listen in yesterday if you've quit? I bet you heard everything, so you know Kip has 'your' part down cold."

"I didn't want to be the only one who didn't know what you guys were doing." Lyndsey tried to defend her eavesdropping. "And Kip won't get to have the part. Trust me, Samantha is so stubborn. Like she thinks she's a genius and nobody can touch her stupid play or change anything."

"I never said that."

We both turned to see Samantha walking behind us, listening to our conversation. Lyndsey looked a little embarrassed, and I wished I had some of Rumpelstiltskin's powers to disappear. Then, almost as good, the bell rang and we all three scattered to class.

Drama at Lunch

I was eating with Kip and Rusty, as usual. They were engrossed in discussing some sci-fi video I hadn't seen yet, so I was sort of humming under my breath, trying not to listen to plot details.

Samantha came up to Lyndsey, Brittani, and their friends at a nearby table, and sat down next to Lyndsey. The others did nothing to hide their surprise. Samantha was breaking the obvious rule of No Group Crossing— going from Geeks to Populars—and without an invitation. I watched them out of the corner of my eye, turning away from Kip and Rusty, pretending to leaf through my binder.

"Lyndsey, I need to explain something to you." Lyndsey gave Samantha a cold look, but didn't try to stop her. "I know you're a real feminist and stuff, but Daffodil's a character in a fairy tale. She's not you personally. Even with the blond wig, nobody's going to get you two confused, believe me. Daffodil's just the not-very-smart daughter of a not-very-smart miller; plus, she's scared. Anyway, if Daffodil could outsmart Rumpelstiltskin when he first shows up, where's the story?"

Ms. Brain has figured it all out, I thought. Too bad she's going to get trashed.

"Okay, fine," said Lyndsey. "Have fun with the idiot daughter. I still quit."

Samantha stood up, keeping her eyes on Lyndsey. "I wish you wouldn't," she said. "You're really good. You're funny and you sing well. And I really don't want a boy to play a girl in my play." She turned and left. I looked at Lyndsey. She kept watching Samantha walk away, even after her friends had started in on how pathetic that poor Geek was.

—

THE NO-SHOWS

Since the show was this week (*aaackk!*), we were having rehearsals every day. We all kept expecting to see Lyndsey—surely she'd made her point and would be back. No such luck.

Our backup Daffodil was nowhere in sight, either. If Mr. C. held out a hope that Kip would return for another rehearsal, it was wasted. I tried appealing to Kip's loyalty to Hope Springs, to theater, and to me. But he would not budge. As soon as school was out, he vanished.

I wondered what Mr. C. planned to do—wait around for Lyndsey?

At rehearsal, Mr. C. made an announcement. "I tried several times last night to reach Lyndsey on the phone, but she was not available." Anyone could see he was being pathetically desperate, breaking his own rule about kicking out anyone who missed the last week of rehearsals. But even people with multiple checks after their names, who should have objected the most, said nothing. So there we were, limping along, Daffodil-less, with Mr. C. reading her part as we rehearsed. Of course, we were awful. Nobody could concentrate, and I think we were all on the verge of giving up.

—

WEDNESDAY: DOWN THE TOILET

In class, Lyndsey made a point of not looking at me or at anyone else who was in the play. But at lunchtime, I accidentally bumped into her as she was coming out of the girls' room.

"Lyndsey!" I said. "Stop. I have to talk to you. The play is going down the toilet without you." She turned around and walked back into the girls' room. I don't know what got into me—I followed her.

"You can't come in here!" She started pushing me.

"I won't leave until you listen to me."

Lyndsey groaned and walked back out. I was very glad to follow her. It was a break for me that nobody else had been in the girls' room. I looked both ways, hoping no one saw me now.

"Okay, what?" she said, marching along in the hall, making me almost run to keep up with her.

"I'll tell you what. You are being really selfish and—and unprofessional." This was not going to get me on her good side, wherever that was, but I was losing patience with her little act.

I plowed ahead. "Mr. C. is a mess. He wants you to come back so bad he's willing to cut you some slack. Come on, I bet . . . I bet he'll even get Samantha to change some of your lines." Oh, boy, I hoped that was true.

"You think so?"

"Sure. I'm positive. Just come to rehearsal this afternoon. You don't have to stay—think of it just as an experiment."

"I don't know. Look, how can I come back now? I mean after all this, you know? It would look like I don't have any principles. Any standards. Like I don't mean what I say."

I pulled at my hair in frustration. "Oh, give me a break! Who are you going to impress by staying away? The antitheater crowd? Certainly not the people who've worked so hard to put on this play." The lunch bell had rung long ago. Lyndsey's speed-walking had taken us to the end of the school, away from the cafeteria. No one was around.

"Look," I continued. "You're a good actor. But being an actor is all about being someone else. Do you think those dudes who play bad guys in movies are really bad in real life?"

Lyndsey rolled her eyes.

"Well, all right," I continued. "They wouldn't get hired if they were. Someone has to be the bad guy. Otherwise, it's one dull movie. Good guy has a great day. Good guy has a great night. The end. Nobody would go to the movies, no more movies would get made, all the actors would be out of work and have to sell their homes and end up moving back to the miserable little towns and cities they came from and end up being petty criminals." I paused, noticing Lyndsey had clamped her hands to her ears and looked like she was about to scream.

"Stop!" she begged. "Do you do this to *everybody* you know or just me?"

"I like to think I don't play favorites."

Lyndsey started walking back the way we came. "That was mostly ridiculous and you know it. But you made one good point. About actors having to play characters they don't approve of—who might be bad or, in this case, idiotic. I guess I should come to rehearsal."

"Excellent! Can I tell the others?"

"No! Just let me show up." She looked sort of embarrassed, which was *not* normal for Lyndsey. "But, the thing is, I don't want to walk in alone, you know? Would you—"

"Sure! No problem. I'll wait for you after seventh period math, okay?"

"Okay. It's a date."

"No, it isn't."

"Duh. I was just joking." She gave me her first smile in a week.

Her Majesty Is Back

"Change some lines?" Samantha sounded like Mr. C. had suggested she cut off a foot.

"I *told* you she wouldn't," Lyndsey said, folding her arms and looking at me.

Her entrance at the start of rehearsal had been as dramatic as I had expected. We walked into the theater and there was this *ahh!* sound. Suddenly everybody stopped talking.

Mr. Caparelli, who had been standing, sat down hard on a stool. "Welcome back, Lyndsey," he said, obviously hoping this wasn't just a visit.

"Thanks," Lyndsey mumbled, looking at the floor.

It's not like people were ready to throw her a party. Now that she was here, it seemed like it was okay to be mad at her for leaving. I heard whispers of "Oh, look, her majesty is back," "Aren't we lucky," "Is she really back or did she just come to yell at us?" That sort of thing.

It looked like no one was going to try to get things on track. Did I have to do *everything?* I said, "Mr. C., Lyndsey told me she's willing to come back if you and Samantha would think about changing some of Daffodil's lines." I sounded like one of those hostage negotiators on TV.

"I don't like actors messing with their lines, Lyndsey," said Mr. C. "But I think we all have a good idea of what's bugging you about Daffodil. And I think you've got a point."

That's when Samantha let us know what she thought about "changing some lines." Now she added, "Change *which* lines?" Samantha was acting like she'd expected Lyndsey back all along and was unimpressed to see her. Hoo boy. This could really backfire.

"I'm willing to allow Daffodil to have a little spunk," said Mr. C. "Maybe not even change any actual *words,* but perhaps let Daffodil stick out her tongue at Rumpelstiltskin when his back is turned, after he has been especially rude."

"Yeah," put in Neesha. "Or have her get all queenlike and haughty when Rumpelstiltskin demands the baby, instead of giggly and forgetful." Both Lyndsey and Samantha gave her a look, but Neesha wasn't bothered by that.

Eventually changes were worked out, mostly involving treating *my* character *worse.* Talk about unfair. After all, I was the one who had returned Lyndsey to the cast. At least the play was still on. I'd still get to wear a beard and be mean.

—

Thursday: Emergency!

Dress rehearsal was on the same night as Molly's school music concert. My parents and Molly had left at 6:00, so she'd be there early to practice and they could get good seats in the front. In *Rumpelstiltskin* world, the Straw was having a special rehearsal at 6:30, but the rest of us didn't start until 7:30. I still had to call Rusty or someone about getting a ride. It was 6:25. Plenty of time to get to that.

Having an excuse to duck Molly's concert had put me in a good mood. We had had breakfast for dinner (a family favorite when we're rushed), and I was still at the kitchen table, munching on my third syrup-soaked waffle and—*finally*—reading the comics from last Sunday. I had worked my way through every strip, even "Prince Valiant" and "Spider Man." As far as I could tell, their stories barely changed from one Sunday to the next. A guy who got punched in one episode would still be falling to the floor three weeks later.

I took another swig of orange juice and leaned forward in the kitchen chair. I had saved the best for last—the "Hocus Focus" panels, where you had to look for what had been changed from picture #1 to picture #2. "At least six things," it always said, in case you were too smart and found an unintended seventh difference. This one was nice and hard, for a change. It showed a kid in a small backyard pool, splashing water on another kid, who was screaming. I was up to five things: the stripes on the pool were wider, the water was more splashy, the screaming kid's arms were higher, the tree was missing, and the gate was wider. Now what was the sixth thing?

I kept losing my concentration because of a repeated

sound, like something tapping against metal. Slowly I looked over the two pictures again, forcing myself not to read the answers below. Maybe it was hair? No, the hair on both kids was the same. Freckles? Noses? The tapping was getting annoying. And now I heard something else. Something like breathing, only weird, like in a monster movie. It was dark outside, and I remembered I was the only person at home. Probably something dumb, but I decided to check before I freaked myself out.

I walked slowly across the kitchen to the laundry room. Standing in the doorway, I looked down the steps and then sucked in a breath. Button was lying on the floor, twitching violently. His foot kept hitting the leg of the ironing board, his claws making the tapping sound. Button's breathing was making the scary noises. His mouth was open slightly and foamy stuff was coming out.

"No!" I whispered. "Oh, Button, no!"

What was happening? I had to do something. Quick. Get Button to the vet. But how? Oh, why was everyone gone? I ran to the window, trying to force my parents to decide to come home now. I even opened the door and looked out. There were no cars in sight, except mean old Mr. Stickle's. Had *everyone* gone to the stupid concert? I rushed back to Button. He was still jerking and breathing hard, raspy breaths. What was wrong? Is this what diabetes did to cats? Or was it something else?

"Why didn't anyone tell me?" I mumbled, as I ran to

the kitchen phone. I looked up the number of the vet on the important numbers list inside the cabinet door. I punched it in. A recording came on, saying the office was closed after 6:00 and giving the number of the emergency veterinary hospital. I had no idea where that was, but I wrote the number down and made the call.

"Animal Emergency, this is Lorna."

I didn't waste time. "It's my cat. Something's really wrong." My voice started out low and then squeaked. The words seemed to be coming from a long way off, from someone else's mouth.

"Can you speak up?" asked the Lorna person. "What's happening with your cat?"

"I don't know. He's all twitchy and jerky and this awful stuff is on his mouth and it's open and he's making this weird sound and I don't know what to do."

"Sounds like you should bring him in," said the Lorna.

"I can't! My mom and dad are out and I can't drive," I said. "I'm only fourteen," I added, in case she thought I was too dumb to learn how.

"Can you call them?" asked Lorna.

"No, they don't have cell phones." My mouth was so dry I could hardly get the words out. "They say cell phones give you brain damage." I was suddenly furious with my parents. What if Button died because they didn't like cell phones?

"Can you get a neighbor to drive?" asked Lorna.

"I don't know," I said. "I'll try." I was afraid I might cry, so I hung up.

Button was the same. Maybe worse. I wiped my eyes and went outside. I looked up and down the street. Mr. Stickle's car was still the only one I could see.

I looked at my watch. It was 6:45. I hadn't called for a ride yet. Rusty. Maybe I could call him, and his mom or dad could take me and Button to the vet? I went back in and dialed his number, but when I got a machine, I hung up. What would I say anyway? Can you take me and my cat to the hospital on your way to rehearsal? It wasn't on the way. And I didn't know his parents. And what if they had already left? "I have to help Button, *now*," I thought, and clenching my fists, I ran outside to Mr. Stickle's house and knocked loudly on the door.

Inside, Mr. Stickle growled, "Who is it?"

Okay, maybe this was *not* a good plan. But I heard myself say, "It's me, Topher Blakely from down the street," all in one breath.

The door opened a crack. "Who?" asked Mr. Stickle again, in a grumpy voice. Then, seeing it was me, he barked, "I told you I'm not buying any tickets, so forget it!"

"Wait," I held up my hand. "I'm not selling anything. I need help. At least my cat does."

"Button?" asked Mr. Stickle.

I nodded, surprised he knew the name.

"What's wrong? Where are your folks?" Mr. Stickle looked over my head toward my house.

I told him. Everything. "So Button's got to go to the emergency vet, fast," I finished.

"Show me the cat," said Mr. Stickle.

—

Horriblest of All

Button was lying still when we got back to him, his mouth still partly open and foamy. Suddenly he started the jerking again. I sucked in a breath.

"We better put him in something," said Mr. Stickle. "What have you got?"

I looked around. The cat carrier was nowhere to be seen, but I spotted a blue plastic laundry basket. I put Button's green cat blanket in it. I hesitated. I hated myself for it, but I couldn't bear to touch Button, all jerky and weird like that. But Mr. Stickle was already leaning down, gently lifting the kitty and placing him on the blanket.

"I'll find the address," said Mr. Stickle, opening the phone book. "You leave a note for your folks."

I wrote something quickly and, carrying the basket with Button, followed Mr. Stickle out of the house.

Mr. Stickle said it would take about twenty minutes to get to the emergency animal hospital. I sat in the backseat, the basket next to me. I felt horrible because

Button was so sick, and horrible for having to miss the important be-there-or-else dress rehearsal, and horriblest of all for being angry at Button for making me miss it.

I kept my eyes glued to Button, as if that would be enough to save him.

—

Stop That Crying

As we drove along, a song from the show was running through my head. It was "Stop That Crying." Concentrating on how stupid it was seemed to help. The trip really did take only twenty minutes, but it seemed like hours before we pulled into the parking lot of the hospital. I carried Button's basket. Mr. Stickle opened the door and went with me up to the counter.

A woman who must have been the Lorna person was typing on a computer.

"I'm Topher Blakely, I called you," I said.

Lorna looked up and immediately came around to the front. "Oh, kitty," she said softly, taking the basket from me. She carried it through a door in the back.

Before I could ask if I should come, too, a man behind the desk started asking a bunch of questions. He needed information about Button—how old he was and when he got diabetes and who his regular vet was and a lot of stuff I really didn't know the answers to. Afterward, Mr. Stickle and I sat in the waiting room chairs, holding magazines. I was kind of glad Mr. Stickle wasn't one for chitchat.

I divided my time between staring at the front of the magazine, which seemed like too much work to open, and checking my watch. It was 7:28, and after a couple of weeks, it was 7:42, and then, about a year later, it was 7:57.

At 8:03, a woman in a doctor coat came out. We stood up. "I'm Dr. Jackson," she said. "We've given Button something to stop the seizures. He's quiet now."

"What was wrong?" I asked.

"Well, it looks like he's had a reaction to the insulin he's been getting. Sometimes cats get so they can't tolerate it, even in low doses."

"What happens next?" asked Mr. Stickle.

"It's possible we can get him to pull through for a little while longer. Maybe a couple more days or weeks," said the vet. "Maybe more. But he'll probably have to come back here or to your regular vet a lot during that time. We suspect he has a tumor as well, but it's hard to tell. We'd need to do some tests."

"So what are you saying? That it's time to put this cat to sleep?" asked Mr. Stickle.

I stared at him, shocked to hear the words I'd been trying not to even think. But I had to hand it to Mr. Stickle. The old guy really didn't care what people thought of him. Even someone he was helping.

"It's up to the family to decide," said Dr. Jackson. "All I can do is give you the information we have."

"He left his folks a note, so we'll wait for them to call," said Mr. Stickle.

That seemed like all there was to do. I didn't want to leave Button, and I sure didn't want to "decide" anything.

At 8:23, Lorna called to me. "Topher? Your dad's on the phone."

I picked it up. "Dad?"

"Hey, son, we just got in and got your message. I'm so sorry you had to deal with this by yourself."

"It's okay." I tried to say Mr. Stickle was helping, but my eyes were stinging and I didn't trust myself not to start crying.

"I'll be over right away," Dad said. "Hang on until I get there."

"Okay." I barely got the word out. I hung up. All my energy was going into not crying. This meant saying only the fewest possible words.

"Do you want to see Button?" asked the vet, as if testing my no-crying policy. "He's calm now. You can sit with him until your dad comes. Then you can both decide what to do."

There it was again. That miserable "decide" word. I knew it meant decide if Button would die now or later. The vet could give him a shot now and end his life, or Dad and I could take Button home and have him around for a little more time, but risk having a cat with seizures and scary stuff that might make him die in pain. What a miserable choice.

I knew one thing for sure. I was never going to be a vet or a doctor or anyone who had to tell people stuff like that every day. It would totally suck.

I realized the vet was still waiting for an answer. "I'll wait until my dad gets here," I said. I glanced at Mr. Stickle, who was standing with his arms folded, looking hard at a poster on the wall about puppy care. As if it was a scene we'd rehearsed, we both sat down, picked up our magazines, and pretended to read.

At 8:46, my dad arrived. He hugged me, and I suddenly got a huge stupid lump in my throat.

"Thanks, Walt," Dad said to Mr. Stickle, shaking his hand, one arm still around me. "This sure goes way beyond neighborly kindness."

Mr. Stickle shrugged. "Kid needed a ride here with the cat. I was home. End of story." He handed me the magazine and left.

Dad talked to the vet, then he took me aside. "If you want my opinion," Dad said, "I think it's best he not suffer anymore. He's had a good life, in cat years."

My heart was screaming, *No! No! No!* But my head wasn't fooled. It knew this was thinking of me, not Button. "Yeah, I guess you're right," I finally said, wiping my hand quickly across my eyes. Stupid tears. "But you tell the doctor lady."

"You bet," said Dad, and walked back to the vet. The two of them talked about cremation and ashes and getting them back in what sort of container. I didn't want any part of that. I stood, holding both my magazine and the one Mr. Stickle had been looking at, and tried to hum to myself to block out the conversation.

"Let's tell Button good-bye now," said Dad, guiding me by the shoulders, not giving me a choice. I didn't want a choice, I didn't want to be here, but here I was.

Dr. Jackson led the way to Button. I was still carrying the magazines, like I was going to read a good article to my cat.

Seeing him lying in the laundry basket, scrawny, hair all matted, he looked like a good candidate for the afterlife. (Sweet dreams. See you in cat heaven.) But he managed a feeble *meow* when Dad and I came in with the vet, and I felt my resolve waver, big time. We both kept our good-byes short. I patted Button's head in a clumsy way, like I'd never touched a cat before. I didn't stay to watch the vet give Button The Shot. I walked out and sat in the car until my dad joined me a few minutes later.

—

AFTER BUTTON

Finally we got home. Mom and Molly were waiting. Dad had called earlier, but still Molly asked, through tears, "Is he dead *now?*"

"Yes. He died quickly and peacefully," said Dad.

"So where did they put him? I mean, is he on some

table or something?" Molly wanted a clear picture, and I wanted to erase all the mental pictures I had of the last few hours.

Dad hugged her. "He's in our old laundry basket, on his old green blanket. We can pick up his ashes in a day or two. Then we can decide what to do with them."

"What do you mean 'pick them up'? Will they be in the basket?" asked Molly, horrified, pulling back from the hug.

"Much nicer than that," said Dad. "And smaller. A wooden box."

"So what do we do with it?" I asked. "Just stick it up on a shelf or something?"

"Let's bury him in the garden," said Molly. She liked calling the random bushes, weeds, and flowers that grew in the backyard "the garden."

"That would be a great place for him," said Mom, getting teary herself. "He had so many favorite sleeping and pooping spots back there."

No one seemed to want to get into burial details just yet. I needed to get away from all of them. I took the portable phone into my room, shut the door, and called Kip.

"Hi. It's me. I have some bad news," I said as soon as Kip answered.

"What, did Mr. C. kick you out?" he asked.

That threw me. "No, why would he do that?"

"Well, I heard from José that you were in trouble for skipping rehearsal. So I was just making a wild guess."

"I didn't *want* to skip rehearsal." I hurried on to avoid more guessing from Kip. "Button's dead."

"Oh, geez. That's awful. I thought he was getting better. What happened?"

I told him the whole story. When I finished, Kip said, "I think I know how you feel. It was so hard when my dog died. I didn't know what to do when I'd get home from school. It was too weird not having her at home to greet me. But it helped to get a new dog."

I hadn't even thought about getting another cat. "I don't see how I could do that," I said. "I mean, I'd want a cat just like Button. A Button clone."

"I say don't get one right away," said Kip. "Remember how we got Charlotte—another retriever—the week after Sheila died? It took me a long time to like her. To not be, like, ticked off at her for being different from Sheila."

There was a knock on my door, and Molly came in before I could answer. She stood in front of me, sort of charged, almost on tiptoe, holding something behind her back.

"I gotta go," I sighed, and hung up.

"I didn't show you my ribbons from Saturday," said Molly.

"What?"

"I got a fourth and a sixth in the show. See?" With a

flourish, she held up the two horseback riding ribbons—one light blue, one green.

"Congratulations, Magoo," I said. I suddenly felt old.

"And look on the back. See? I've dedicated them to Button," she said.

In the circle of space where the name of the horse, rider, and judge usually went, some serious erasing had gone on. Instead, written neatly in ink, on both ribbons, was: *In memory of Button Blakely.*

"Cool," I said, nodding solemnly. I couldn't think of anything else to say. This was about as pointless as dedicating a report card to your dead pet. But, I reminded myself, horses were at the center of Molly's universe.

"I know Button wasn't exactly into horses," Molly added, as if most cats were.

"Well, I'm sure he would have approved." It was all I could think of to say.

Mom came in to tell us we really needed to get to bed, since it was a school day tomorrow. Molly said we shouldn't have to go to school right after Button had died, but Mom did not agree.

All at once, I thought of the missed dress rehearsal and what Kip had said. Showing mind-reading skills, Mom told me Mr. Caparelli had called tonight from the theater and had left a message asking why I wasn't at dress rehearsal.

"Don't worry," she said, seeing my look of despair. "I

called him back. I told him what was going on. He was very understanding. But he wants you to come by his classroom tomorrow morning before school so he can tell you about some staging changes."

I just nodded, and got ready for bed. Brushing my teeth, changing into my pajamas, saying good night—I did it all in zombie mode. But climbing into my bed, out of habit, I looked to see if Button was sleeping on it. And then everything seemed to hit me at once. I turned out the light and really did cry.

—

Friday: Opening Night

"What do you mean you need tights and black dance shoes by *tonight?*" Mom did not take my announcement well.

"Look, I'm sorry Mom, I just forgot. And since I missed the big dress rehearsal . . ." I was only a little ashamed to use Button's Last Day as an excuse for having spaced on the tights and shoes weeks before. It worked like a charm.

"Okay, honey, I'll see what I can find," said Mom, calming down and heading for her bedroom. She came back only a few minutes later with a pair of black shoes and black tights.

"Wow, Mom, that was fast!" I was amazed.

"Try these," she said, handing them to me. "The shoes are mine—from when I took that modern dance class. I think our feet are about the same size. And the tights are Molly's, but they're new. I think they're a little long for her." She looked around, like maybe we were being spied on. Then she whispered, "Just don't tell her. I'll get her some more."

I went to my bedroom and tried on the shoes. They were a little big, but they would do. I didn't feel like trying on the tights. Actually, I didn't feel like wearing tights at all, but I didn't have a choice.

All day, school had been royally weird. Not the part about talking to Mr. C. That went fine, and he explained some staging changes that had been worked out. But kids kept coming up to me to ask if I'd been kicked out and who would be Rumpelstiltskin and did Kip know that part, too? It was highly annoying, and I was feeling more and more tense. I have no idea what went on in my classes. My body showed up, but my brain was in the theater, practicing the changes Mr. C. had told me about, and panicking. I'm not even sure how I got home.

In a flash, it was 6:15, and Dad drove me back to Hope Springs. The show started at 8:00, but the cast and tech crew had to be at the auditorium by 6:30. The whole way there, Dad tried to get me to eat the sandwich he'd brought.

"You'll be starving by intermission and you'll need the energy," he urged.

I could not imagine forcing the tiniest bite of anything into my mouth right now. Even if I did, I was so nervous I had no idea how I'd be able to swallow it. Lines from the play kept swirling around in my head, mixing with the wrong tunes.

I tried to distract myself. A passenger in a pickup truck in front of us spit out the window. It landed in a shiny glob on the asphalt. I craned my neck to see if our wheels would touch it. They missed, but the car behind us rolled right over the spit. For some reason this was comforting. A direct hit. A good omen. I was desperate for good omens right about then.

Backstage, the boys' and girls' dressing areas were separated by a narrow passageway with a couch, a Kleenex-flowered archway for the palace garden, and the props table. Everything anyone had to carry onstage was in a specially marked spot on this table. Kids hung out on the couch when they weren't due on stage for a while.

By the time Mr. Caparelli had given everyone last-minute notes and Ms. Lopez had gone over a couple of the songs, it was time to get in costume. I could hear the audience starting to arrive. I tried to guess from the sound how many people were actually there.

I'd heard it was sold out, but what if a lot of people decided it sounded like a weird show? What if they changed their minds and didn't come? What if there was a line of people right now, trying to sell back their tickets? What if there was no one in the audience tomorrow night and Sunday? It could mean the end of the drama program at Hope Springs forever. This cast full of dorks in a stupid play would be held up as the reason for the failure of The Arts in our town for all eternity.

My runaway imagination was pulled back by Mr. Caparelli. "Act one, scene one, onstage, now! Curtain in ten minutes."

Tight Tights

I got into my costume.

Turtleneck.

Tunic.

Beard

Hat.

Now for the tights. They looked awfully short. Well, they would probably stretch. I stuck both feet in and started to pull them on. The waist was really tight. I could hardly breathe as I leaned over, ready to put on my shoes. Oh, great. The crotch came only a few inches above my knees. No amount of pulling could get the crotch any higher. I gave the tights one final tug, stretching out my feet, and a hole popped open in the left leg, right at my knee.

Ms. Lopez played the opening music—a medley of the songs in the play—which was followed by the enthusiastic applause of an audience packed with parents. The first act began. Samantha, Lyndsey, and José were onstage. I peeked outside the dressing-area curtain. The Guards were waiting in the wings; the King and the Straw were lined up to follow them after the second song. I waddled out into the passageway and tiptoed up to Rusty, the only other actor who had to wear tights.

"Hey," I whispered. "Do you have any spare tights? Mine are too small." Several members of the Straw turned and looked at me. They started giggling.

"Whoa, dude, those look really dumb," Rusty whispered back, patting his fake red moustache and rocking with suppressed laugher.

"No kidding," I scowled. "Look, I need tights—do you have any?"

Onstage, the Miller was well into "Tell the King About My Talented Girl." The next scene would start soon.

"Ask Michael's mom. She's in charge of costumes," Rusty suggested.

I waddled off and found Michael's mom, helping a Straw shut the back of his costume with Velcro.

"I think I might need a new pair of tights," I whispered.

"We don't have any extra tights," said Michael's mom. She looked down at my legs. "Those are a mess! Why didn't you get a pair that fit?"

Because I like looking like an idiot, I wanted to snap, but I just sighed and worked my way back to the others.

One of the girls, Caitlyn, broke away from the Straw pack and tiptoe-ran to the girls' dressing area. She came back a moment later waving something with legs. "You can wear these. I'm not allowed to wear them with this costume." She said it a little wistfully. She was smiling, holding out a pair of tights.

I looked at them. They were tights. They were long. And they were lime green and hot pink. Big wide stripes of lime green and hot pink. Who wore stuff like this? Was it even legal to sell it?

"Uh, thanks a lot," I said. Caitlyn was smiling and holding out the tights. I didn't want to be rude and turn down the offer in front of everyone, so I took the tights and walked back to the dressing area. There I mentally reviewed my options.

Option 1. Don't wear any tights at all. Results: Comfortable, but ugly, due to hairy white legs. Major risk of underwear showing.

Option 2. Wear the striped tights. Results: Comfortable, but a look that would start the wrong kind of laughs rolling for years.

Option 3. Stay with the black tights. Results: Hideously uncomfortable with a growing hole in one knee, but okay with the black shoes. And since I had to hunch down for the part anyway, maybe I could keep people from noticing the low level of the crotch.

Option three had to be it. Just as well—I wouldn't have to change. I didn't want to practice hunching around backstage, for fear of making the hole worse.

Better Than Christmas

Soon I heard Lyndsey finishing up "Woe Is Me." Time for my entrance. Wondering if all the people in the first two rows could hear my heart pounding, I took a deep breath. Then, giving the tights a final tug, I straightened my beard, adjusted my hat, and, hunching over, I leaped out onto the stage.

"Stop that crying!" I commanded. *"I hate crying—hate it hate it hate it!"*

There was a burst of laughter. The music began, and I plunged ahead with "Stop That Crying." I waved my arms and stomped around the whole time, managing to stay stooped over. The tights were the definition of uncomfortable.

The performance continued:

> Daffodil: Oh my! You frightened me!
>
> Rumpelstiltskin: Frightened? The only thing
>   you need to fear is someone lighting
>   a match to all that straw.
>
> (Whimpering from the Straw.)
>
>   So why are you crying?
>
> Daffodil: Because I have to spin all this straw
>   into gold by morning or—get this—the
>   King will cut off my head!

We went on from there, to the part about Daffodil giving Rumpelstiltskin her necklace as payment. I started to stuff the necklace into my pocket. Or tried to, but I suddenly noticed I didn't have a pocket. After a bit of fumbling, I stuffed it into my shoe.

The hole in the tights expanded and the crotch lowered even further. The waistband was now about halfway down my butt. I pulled to make sure my tunic was still covering my behind. With a low and crablike gait, I worked my way over to the spinning-wheel bench.

I spun the bicycle-tire spinning wheel and started to hum tunelessly as usual, when I remembered the magical incantation I'd worked out last night. Lying in bed, fighting against my mental pictures of Button having the seizures, and thoughts of possible opening-night disasters, getting to sleep had been impossible. Eventually, I'd remembered the conversation with Mom. Working out a "magical incantation" had given me something *real* to do. I tried it under my breath:

> *Darkest stroganoff!*
> *Blackest tea!*
> *Butter light and elephant pee!*
> *Now just straw, but gold to be!*

That was about as magical as I was ever going to get. I mumbled it over and over, holding Straw-representative Neil's arm near the wheel. I pulled on his sleeve, which came away in my hand as it was supposed to, revealing Neil's gold-colored T-shirt.

Meanwhile, Lyndsey had yawned and slumped to the

floor, faking a good imitation of sleep. One by one, the Straw took off their outer costumes, turning into Gold as they sang "We Were Straw, But Now We're Gold," to the tune of "Camp Town Races."

When it was time for my exit, I hobbled offstage and immediately took the sharp, lumpy necklace out of my shoe. I remembered to put it on the props table. Then I watched from the wings. I was looking, but all I heard in my head were the giggles and laughter that had come from the audience at the funny stuff I had done onstage. It was better than Christmas.

Rusty, as the King, entered again and did a fine double take when he saw all the artfully arranged Gold before him. Soon he was singing "A Miracle, I Must See More," and I switched my full attention to the stage. I was laughing, too, when Rusty leaned forward, while singing about cutting off Daffodil's head, and dramatically kissed the top of her curly blond wig.

The costume mom showed me how I could try to make the tights go higher up my legs by pulling up tiny bits of material, a little at a time, starting at my ankles. It did manage to gain slightly more stretch, so the top was back near my waist. But the hole was even bigger now.

I finished just as the Gold came offstage, "carried" by the Guards. They immediately put their straw costumes back on, and returned to the stage, once again with the Guards. They were accompanied by the Second Pile of

Straw cast. The King finished challenging poor Daffodil to the second impossible task, and then Rusty came off-stage with a swish of his cloak, looking pleased with himself.

"Way to go!" I whispered. Then I squinted at Rusty. Something was different, but I couldn't think what.

Lyndsey went into a reprise of Daffodil's pathetic song. Waiting in the wings, I noticed she was wearing an odd decoration in her hair that hadn't been there before. At least I was pretty sure it hadn't. It looked like a fuzzy red bow, and it was stuck to the bangs of her wig.

But in a moment, I was back onstage, demanding to know if Daffodil had forgotten I hated crying. I hunched around, gesturing at the new, bigger pile of Straw. When we got to the part where Rumpelstiltskin demands another valuable item in exchange for more spinning magic, Daffodil took off her ring and handed it to me. I reached toward her to take it and then paused.

I recognized what was now dangling from her wig. It was the King's mustache. It must have stuck there when he kissed her hair. As I took the ring with one hand, I tried to casually grab the wayward mustache with the other. Lyndsey pulled back in surprise at having me touch her head, and the mustache, attached now by just a hair, swung back and forth before her eyes. Seeing it, Lyndsey gave a little shriek, pulling it off and flinging it to the floor.

The audience went wild. For a moment, Lyndsey and I stood frozen, staring at the fuzzy red object. Thinking fast, I leaned over and grabbed the mustache, saying, "Ah! My pet red spider! I wondered where it was." But now what? I couldn't exactly wear it. I ended up stuffing both mustache and ring in my shoe. There was a collective *Eewww!* from the audience. I turned to them. "Don't worry," I said, still in my Rumpelstiltskin voice. "He likes it there."

As soon as I came offstage, I reached into my shoe and handed the mustache to Rusty, who was about to go back on. "I can't put that on my *lip!*" whispered Rusty, holding the mustache at arm's length. "You've had it in your shoe! It's probably got your toe jam on it!"

"So wash it, and you're welcome, your royal fartness." I figured I was due a little thanks for saving the scene.

"Your entrance, King, *now*," prompted Mr. Caparelli.

Rusty tossed the mustache back at me and grinned. "Looks like the King had a shave," he said as he swept onto the stage, demanding for the third and final time to see the gold.

The rest of the first act went pretty well. Only a few newly transformed Golds were still tugging off their straw decorations when the King reappeared. Rumpelstiltskin was the only character not on stage for The Wedding Dance. Everyone was singing the ridiculous

"Oh, Happy Day," sung to the tune of the theme from "Sesame Street." Dorky as that scene was, I missed being out there.

—

Intermission

Between acts, we were supposed to stay backstage, out of sight of the audience. But most kids tried to peek through the curtains or go around to the side to get someone from the audience to buy them one of the immense chocolate chip cookies on sale in the lobby. I was no exception. I spotted Molly near the front of the line.

"Pssst! Molly!" I got her attention and waved a dollar at her. "Get me a cookie, would you?"

Molly got a friend to hold her place in line and ran over to me. "You're doing great, Topher! But what's with the tights? They look awful. Where'd you get them?"

"Uh, Mom gave them to me." I was anxious to change the subject. "Come on, will you get me a cookie? Here's a dollar."

"Okay. Too bad they're not selling tights." Molly got back in line and bought me a cookie. Just in time, too, because a backstage dad was coming around to enforce the no-talking-to-the-audience rule.

—

A Hole in the Floor

No one seemed to have left before the second act, and I was feeling more confident all the time. I was looking forward to the climax, my stomping scene. Hitching up the disintegrating tights once more, I headed onstage to confront Daffodil with her baby. No longer a wadded-up sweatshirt, the baby was now a doll, wrapped in a yellow blanket. Daffodil held it in her lap, as she sat in a garden outside the palace.

It all went fairly smoothly, with only a couple of mixed-up lines on Rumpelstiltskin's first and second visits, when Lyndsey and I were working our way through the names Daffodil was guessing. However, as the third and final time approached, the thought of Kip as Daffodil popped into my head, and I got nervous again. Oh, no. Could I do the scene without cracking up?

Daffodil: Is it . . . Rum—pel—stilt—skin?

Rumpelstiltskin: Who *told* you? You *cheated*,

I *know* you did!

The plan was for me to do my stomping and yelling and then, on the final stomp, I would shriek and the lights would go out. Of course I wouldn't make a *real* hole in the floor, but by moving a covered table to one side, and hiding under it, I would reveal a painted "hole" where the table had been, plus get myself out of sight at the same time. Then the lights would come back up. It would be dark for only three seconds. Three seconds was all the time I would have.

I was stoked—I'd avoided cracking up at Daffodil's lines. Now, as I carefully followed all the stomping stage directions, my face actually felt hot and red, and I'm sure a wild look came into my eyes. The audience was screaming with laughter.

But I realized with a sudden sense of doom that this was not a result of my fine acting skills. It was the tights. With every stomp, they were inching their way down my butt, faster than ever before. I nearly toppled over as I stomped my final stomp and then shrieked my final "*AAAchhhk!*" With a ping of release, the waistband broke and the tights collapsed around my ankles.

—

Curtain Call!

But the Gods of Theater—or at least the tech crew—were with me. In the split second before this occurred, the stage went dark, right on cue. There was the rumble of "thunder"—as a drum rolled and cymbals crashed—and I moved the table and scrambled under the long cloth covering it just as the lights came back up again. My red hat fell off, and I didn't have time to place it next to the "hole." But at least it was nearby.

Samantha had the last lines: "*The King and Queen lived happily ever after, and no one ever saw Rumpelstiltskin again.*"

The music of the finale started up, and so did I. Blocked from view by a chorus line of returning Gold, I wriggled my way offstage through the back curtain. There, I took off my shoes, peeled off the offending tights, dashed to my dressing area, threw on my jeans, and made it back onstage just in time for the bows.

My first curtain call as the male lead! To come onstage last to bow, just me and Lyndsey—I can't explain the rush. I thought my chest was going to pop.

And the way everyone behind us was clapping and cheering, too, it was as if we had always been a tight team. All the arguing and crabby comments and fears it would flop and Lyndsey quitting hadn't been real. *This* was real. The rest melted away. I was ready to do this all over again. From scratch. A musical of "The Three Blind Mice"? Show me where I sign up. The story of the Dewey decimal system? Bring it on.

It was over in a flash, but I had saved it to my inner hard drive so I could revisit that moment, and all my favorites from the night, over and over.

—

Cold Chocolate Fear II

After the show, Mom and Dad took me, Kip, and Molly and her two friends out for ice cream. The Chosen Frozen was crowded, but, in an unexpected flash of understanding, my parents sat at the counter and let us kids take the last booth.

When our ice cream cones came, Kip and I explained to the girls how the aliens in *Cold Chocolate Fear* killed people.

"Say these are the people," I said, pinching two tiny

chocolate jimmies between my thumb and forefinger. "Help! Help! It's coming!!" I squealed in a high voice. The place was really loud, but still, a couple of people turned to stare for a moment.

"Eww," said Molly. "That is just stupid." But she and her friends were giggling.

We kept examining our cones, claiming to see people the girls knew, then shrieking demonically and licking the ice cream. We had them all laughing pretty hard, when suddenly Kip gave me a vicious kick under the table. I was about to pound him, but looked up. Daniel Brickster was standing by the booth with his pals, Eric of the too-close eyes and Jack of the already-deep voice.

"Hey, T-man, hanging with the diaper set?" Daniel said, glancing with mock amusement at Molly and her friends. "Do your little dates know they're out with fairies?"

"This is my sister, *jerkwad*," I blurted, then immediately wished I hadn't.

"Well *that* makes it all clear," laughed Daniel.

I racked my brain for *something* in my arsenal of cutting retorts, but I was coming up empty. Again. Daniel had turned from our table and was yukking it up with Eric and Jack, who had been scanning the room for seats.

"So, would those three guys be what you meant by 'Losers'?" Molly gestured toward them, sounding like she was trying to identify unusual insects. Kip gave me a look. Eric turned his head. Had he heard this last part? My life was ready to flash before my eyes. Then a table must have opened up because they hurried off.

Sounding as relieved as I was, Kip said, "Good eyes, Molly. Those are definitely Losers."

Molly wasn't done. "Would you say Regular Losers or Scary Losers?"

"What do you think?" I rolled my eyes at her. I was torn between feeling proud and wishing she'd shut up.

Mom and Dad came over right after that to say it was time to go.

"Who were those boys?" asked Mom on the way out, looking over at Daniel, Eric, and Jack sitting in a booth by the window. "Were they in the play?"

"Why don't I go over and ask them?" suggested Molly. But I clamped my hand over her mouth.

"Topher, stop! That's uncalled for!" said Dad.

"I have to do it, Dad," I answered. "It's a life-saving move."

But I let go of Molly. Both my parents were looking confused. Finally we got out of the Chosen Frozen and safely into the car.

We laughed and goofed around all the way home, and everybody talked about how great the show had been and how funny my tights were.

But as soon as I walked into the house, I caught

myself looking for Button, and his absence was a worse
punch than the one I'd almost expected from Daniel. All
I wanted was to go to bed with my cat next to me,
purring his fool head off.

—

Button's Ashes

Saturday afternoon, Dad came home with a small box.
"Here's Button," he announced. "I mean to say, here are
his ashes."

We crowded around to see the box. It was wooden,
wrapped once with a cord tied in a bow.

"It's so pretty," said Mom.

"It's so small," said Molly.

"Yeah," I agreed. "I thought it would be bigger."

Nobody seemed to want to hold it, so Dad put it on
the mantelpiece.

"You kids can bury the box tomorrow in the backyard," he said.

—

Saturday Night: Smooth as Silk

Mom had bought me two pairs of excellent black tights
that fit fine—not too short, not too long. The whole play,
and especially the stomping scene, went smooth as silk.

After the show, the cast came out into the lobby so we
could say hi to any friends and family who'd come. Some
people got flowers. I was talking to Lyndsey's parents,
when a man I didn't know came up to me. He looked

too young to be someone's dad, but you could never be sure with adults.

"Great job, Topher," he said, holding out his hand. "You are one funny guy."

I shook it, somewhat awkwardly. Who *was* this guy?

I guess he could tell I was clueless about him. He smiled. "Here's a hint. Lemonade stand? Last ticket to sell?"

"Oh! You're the dude on the bike! Wow. I gotta tell my sister."

—

Sunday: Final Performance

When the Sunday matinee rolled around, everyone was getting pretty punchy. We were exhausted from the high of performing and, for days, nobody had had enough sleep. The sweet relief of realizing the production was not a bomb had given way to an energy slump. Several members of the cast arrived late or wandered around aimlessly once they were backstage. Costumes were starting to rip and some props needed patching. Neesha's royal guard cape was attached by a parade of tiny safety pins, and Rusty was using duct tape to keep his crown together. Mr. C., however, was holding together quite nicely. He was relaxed enough about the way things were going to sit in the audience with Samantha's family. He beamed expectantly at the stage.

Backstage, I had carefully pulled on my tights for the

last time (why would anyone wear these things on purpose?). I was adjusting my beard in front of the mirror by the couch, when I noticed someone curled up with a script over her face. It was Lyndsey.

"Hey, Daffinatious, no naps allowed. It's show time!" I teased, giving her a nudge. Lyndsey groaned and dragged herself to her feet. Her skin was pale, she seemed to be sort of sweaty, and the whites of her eyes had switched to red. She reminded me of Molly the week she'd had the flu.

"Geez!" I said. "Are you sick?"

"No, I'm okay, probably," said Lyndsey, without much conviction. She squinted at the script she was holding. "Topher. You know that scene? The one . . . the one with the second pile of straw? There's a place we need to go over. Where we both get the lines mixed up all the time . . . and, um, where is it?" She turned pages, slowly sinking back down onto the couch. I waited a while, but she seemed to have lost track of what she wanted to say, so I left her alone.

I found the peephole in the side curtain and looked into the auditorium. It was satisfyingly full. I spotted my parents near the front. And there was Kip, seated in a back row with a few kids from English class. I considered waving, but thought better of it. One of the backstage parents came by, giving the Ten Minutes to Curtain warning.

Someone touched my arm. "There you are," Lyndsey whispered, grimly. "I told you we have to go over that second straw-pile scene."

"We don't have time now," I pointed out. "Anyway, it'll be fine. And you need to take it easy."

I expected an argument, but she only sighed and walked away.

Soon the house lights went down, and Ms. Lopez started the Overture, giving it more energy than ever. White as a sheet and looking as if even walking hurt, Lyndsey took her place onstage, on the bench next to José. I was beginning to doubt she could make it through the first scene, much less the whole show.

And if she dropped out, who could read her part? Of course Samantha knew the lines, though maybe not from memory, but she had to be the Narrator. In fact, she was walking onstage now, ready to stand in front of the curtain and say something about writing this play and the history of fairy tales. Maybe one of the Straws or even some random backstage parent would end up holding a script and reading Daffodil's lines. It would be a disaster. Nobody but Lyndsey was prepared to do that role.

Well, almost nobody.

—

ACT I

I made a decision. I tiptoed upstairs and around to the back of the auditorium.

The curtain rose. Onstage, Samantha finished the introduction and then Lyndsey and José started in about their boring, nowhere lives and how they deserved better than to be stuck in a nowhere town, working a mill. Lyndsey's voice was almost inaudible as she sang her part of "We Are So Unimportant." Michael and Neesha, the two Guards out doing errands for the King, waited in the wings for their cue to enter and ask for a drink of water.

Keeping on the lookout for backstage parents, I tiptoed through the dimly lit lobby, and entered at the rear of the darkened theater. Crouching low, I crept over to Kip's row and I poked him from behind to get his attention. He turned, both confused and annoyed, but slid out of the row. We retraced my steps until we were backstage in the dressing area.

"What's going on, Toph?"

"It's an emergency," I whispered. "I need you to do me the hugest favor of our entire lives. Lyndsey's sick—and I don't mean sorta-got-a-headache sick, I mean major-puke-on-the-way sick. I don't think she'll make it through this scene, much less the whole show. You've got to go on for her—you're the only one who knows Daffodil's lines."

Kip gaped at me. "Are you nuts? I can't do that. No way." He started to walk back.

"Wait, wait!" I grabbed his arm. "Why? Give me one

good reason. I mean one that's more important than saving this show."

"I'll give you three. One, did you notice I'm not a girl? Two, you know I hate acting in front of a crowd. Three, did you see who is in the audience? That's right, Daniel and company. Plus, I bet I *don't* know all the lines."

"That's four."

"Okay, bonus reason. Look, there's no way I'm doing this."

We heard a backstage parent coming along, no doubt to investigate the loud whispers. I looked around, grabbed a Straw's hat and jammed it on Kip's head. Then I pretended to adjust my beard and Kip leaned over to check his shoelaces. The backstage parent kept walking. Onstage, the Miller and the Guards went into "Tell the King About My Talented Girl," and Lyndsey left to get the two cups of water for the Guards.

"She looks fine to me," Kip started to complain, taking off the hat. But as soon as Lyndsey stepped offstage, she started running. She only got as far as the props table and promptly threw up on the baby doll. There was a scurry of activity as backstage parents rushed to help her and clean up.

Onstage, unaware of what was happening, the singers continued.

I knew I had to act fast, before Mr. Caparelli figured something had gone wrong and took drastic action, like reading Lyndsey's part himself. I grabbed Kip's arm and we raced to Lyndsey's dressing area, brushing aside the backstage parents trying to keep us away, with a "Mr. C. sent us." Not true, but I was sure Mr. C. *would* have sent us, if he knew the plan.

"Lyndsey!" I whispered into the dressing area curtain. "Give me your wig! And any costume you can spare. Ki— . . . uh, there's someone who can go on for you." There was some mumbling, and then a hand reached out holding the wig of curly blond hair and a long skirt. "Thanks!" I snatched them and put the skirt over Kip's head.

"Stop it!" he hissed. "I never said I'd do this!"

I worked fast, pulling the skirt down to his waist, ignoring his wriggling protests, until he finally broke away. We both froze and just stared at each other. It was like some face-off in a Western movie.

Onstage the song was over. Confused actors waited for Daffodil to return with the cups of water.

And waited.

"So. Come this way often?" ad-libbed the Miller to the Guards, stalling for time. All three kept glancing nervously toward the wings.

"Oh, once in a while," said Guard Neesha, pitching in to help. There was another awkward pause.

Backstage, I stood looking at Kip, the wig in my hand. Finally he snatched it from me and jammed it on his head. I gave a huge sigh of relief.

134

Onstage, José the Miller tried again. "Um, sure is hot today, don't you think?"

"Yeah, especially in this uniform. . . ." Guard Neesha's voice trailed off.

Guard Michael said nothing, standing frozen to his spot, waiting for rescue.

I was thumbing furiously through a script I'd picked up while Kip adjusted the skirt. "Okay, here. Your next line is '*Here you go! Cool water from our well.*' Remember that part?"

"Yeah . . . Then it's '*What's the King really like?*' right?"

"Right! Okay, go!" I almost shoved him onto the stage, just as Mr. Caparelli was rising from his seat. There was Kip, entering in Daffodil's wig and skirt, carrying the cups. Staring in disbelief, Mr. C. sat back down. Or rather, he seemed to sink into his chair.

Kip waltzed in with the cups and, in a high voice, said, "*Here you go! Cool water from our well. Sorry it took me so long.*"

The audience gasped, then burst out laughing.

Seeing Kip, wig and all, the other actors froze for a moment. I could actually tell that Samantha, in the Narrator's corner, was shaking all over. No doubt she was torn between staying put, because "the show must go on," and ripping Kip limb from limb.

Finally Neesha took one of the cups, pretended to drink, and then elbowed Michael to do the same. He was still staring at Kip, like he was seeing a ghost, so he was late with his line. Suddenly remembering it, he grabbed the cup and blurted, *"Miller, you have a pretty wench for a daughter!"*

Of course this started the audience howling again and Kip had to repeat his line, *"What's the King really like?"* twice before he could be heard.

From the wings, I saw Mr. Caparelli excusing himself and working his way to the end of his row. Onstage, the actors forged ahead. While the Miller and Daffodil hung out on their bench, stage left, the Guards returned to the royal palace, stage right.

Rusty the King entered, and they told him all about the Miller's remarkable gold-spinning daughter. He demanded to see her at once. The new Daffodil—wearing an oversized blond wig, long flowered skirt, and black "Go Giants" T-shirt—and her father were presented to the King.

Backstage, Mr. Caparelli greeted us with a harsh whisper. "What happened to Lyndsey?"

"Sick," I whispered back, and led him to the girls' dressing area, where Mr. C. talked in low whispers with a couple of backstage parents, who pointed once at me. I couldn't hear what anyone was saying. I wanted desperately to give my side of things, but I couldn't afford to miss my first cue.

Just then, Lyndsey's mom arrived to take her home.

Mr. C. talked to her a minute, and at one point, I heard him say, "At least it didn't happen on opening night."

A chalky-pale Lyndsey came out of the dressing room. She held on to her mother's arm, but instead of leaving, looked around, and then came up to me. "Here," she whispered. "He's going to need these." Then she handed me the ring and the necklace.

"Oh! Thanks!" I whispered back, but she was already heading for the door. I looked at the jewelry in my hand. I had completely forgotten about this detail. Daffodil wouldn't be coming offstage before she—or rather *he*—would need these. What to do? I had to come up with a plan, pronto. Kip was singing "Woe Is Me," and I was due onstage in seconds. Would I have to give him this stuff *myself?*

I saw Neesha about to go on. "Wait!" I ran up, grabbing her arm. She gave me a look like she was going to deck me. I thrust the necklace and ring into her hand, curling her fingers around them. "You gotta give these to Kip."

Neesha looked at her hand, said nothing, and went onstage with Michael and the Straw.

As the Guards pushed the Straw into place, I held my breath. Was Neesha going to hand the ring and necklace to Kip? *Could* she? Or was she simply thinking up a way to strangle me with these new weapons? But I should have known I picked the right kid for the job. Once again, Neesha proved herself a master of improvisation.

Nothing sneaky about Neesha. Instead of exiting with Rusty and Michael, she walked over to a weepy Daffodil and handed the jewelry to "her" with a flourish.

"Here. You may keep these after all," she said, as if taking them away had really been part of some earlier scene.

Kip proved to be up to the challenge. He sniffed dramatically and ad-libbed, "Oh, I take comfort in my only treasures!" He put them on, and Neesha marched offstage. Moments later, Kip was pretending to sob and I was entering with my angry order for Daffodil to *"stop that crying!"*

—

Intermission: Explain This One

Backstage, Samantha demanded, and got, a full explanation from me and Kip.

"How do I know you guys didn't set up this whole thing with Lyndsey, just to ruin my play?"

If a picture is worth a thousand words, so is a smell. I located the barfed-on baby doll in a paper bag under the props table. (Apparently each of the backstage parents had been hoping someone else was going to clean it.) I brought it over to Samantha. She didn't even have to open it.

"Poor Lyndsey!" she said. "Geez, I *thought* she was looking really pale out there earlier." Samantha looked at Kip. "Not my first choice, but thanks for pitching in. You are getting maximum laughs, that's for sure. We all owe you big for this."

"No kidding," said Kip. "Just pay me back by never dragging me onstage again." He was smiling, but I knew he meant it.

Act II

I was helping Kip put on the retired prom dress that served as Daffodil's gown, now that she was a queen. It was rather tight across his shoulders and forced him to hunch forward like he was cold. The wig was mashed farther down on his head by a plastic tiara crown.

"Okay," I said, "Now you need the baby and the basket. Has anyone cleaned them yet?"

Someone had. Sort of. Samantha earned herself major points by volunteering to take the doll, blanket, and basket to the girls' room sink, where she had quickly rinsed and washed them with liquid hand soap. Now she hurried over with them. Bits of paper towel were still sticking to the sides of the basket and the doll's hair. The blanket, which had taken the biggest hit, was still very wet.

Samantha looked grim. She wrapped the drippy, smelly doll in the even drippier, smellier blanket, popped them in the basket, and handed it to Kip. "We have to be onstage *now*," she said, and pulled him into place just before the curtain went up.

Watching from the opposite wings, I saw that the new

Daffodil, instead of smiling with motherly tenderness, looked positively repulsed by her baby. Not only were the baby and its blanket wet, but a puddle was forming on the floor under them. But that was not the worst part. The worst part was the smell. The hurried washing with a little soap and lots of water had washed off the chunks, but the odor remained. The audience probably didn't smell anything. It just looked like this baby needed a diaper change in the worst way.

When I got onstage and had Rumpelstiltskin demand the sopping-wet baby as payment, it looked like Daffodil might be only too willing to give it up. Instead of clasping it to his chest to protect it, Kip held the doll at arm's length, like it might be a ticking bomb, and rocked it awkwardly, with an up-and-down pumping motion.

In spite of this latest challenge, Kip was doing famously. When he forgot a line or two, he knew the play well enough to make something up that was close. Fortunately, Rusty went right along with it and didn't freak when he wasn't handed the right line for his response.

If it had been hard for me not to crack up when I was practicing the stomping scene with Kip doing Daffodil, it was now all I could do to hold myself together with him being Daffodil *in costume*. I had to try to go to some inner Zen place of detachment or whatever it is my mom says she's trying to do when Molly and I are fighting.

Once Kip got into being Daffodil—really cut loose

and expressed his inner brainless twit—he was unstoppable. Nothing Lyndsey had ever done could compare with the laughs he was pulling out of every line. It was Academy Award stuff, and it was all I could do to keep up. Rusty, too. I could tell he was working hard to stay in character and not dissolve in a laughing fit. It's possible Kip was going a bit over the top, but why not? With Daniel out there, this could be his last day on Earth, not to mention his one and only performance onstage.

Backstage again, I looked out at the audience, wondering how Mr. Caparelli was taking all this. The director was back in his seat, a look of amazement on his face. But he was laughing and clapping and seemed to be having as much fun as anyone.

At the final curtain, Kip swept off the wig like it was a hat and bowed deeply. The audience went nuts. Mr. C. came onstage and held up his hands for quiet. "Thank you for attending a most unusual final performance . . ." (more laughter) "of *Rumpelstiltskin*, written by our contest winner, Samantha Reynolds." (More clapping.)

Samantha smiled and bowed.

"As you may have guessed," continued Mr. C., "our original Daffodil took ill after the first scene. Mr. Kip Cohen kindly agreed to take her place without notice. I think he has done a splendid job." Kip took another bow, his face pretty red.

It took a while for Mr. Caparelli to calm everyone down again so he could continue. "I am pleased to announce that the PTA has been able to come up with the funds to produce a *second* play, in the spring. It turns out the first runner-up in our contest was Kip's own original script, *The Sweet Tooth of Death*. So we will present that detective thriller in a rare *spring* semester production."

I whooped, and joined everyone giving high fives to a surprised and overwhelmed Kip.

—

Act Normal

Before the cast party, we all had to help strike the sets and generally clean up. Finally, Mom and Dad could give Kip and me a ride to the party.

"Is that cool or what!" I was grinning so hard at Kip my cheeks hurt. "Of course, you're going to be in your own play, aren't you?"

"'Of course' nothing!" Kip looked appalled. "You know I hate acting in front of a lot of people."

"But it's *your* play!" I practically shouted. "You're a natural actor. You've got to be in it."

"Only if I can be the director," smiled Kip.

The cast party was the usual dud. Kids stood around in an overbright room, the walls lined with adults expecting trouble, a TV running with a student-made video of the play that was too dark and that no one could actually hear.

After a while, pizza arrived. The two of us ate some and then, to entertain ourselves, poured a little soda on squares of cake, which we stirred into a mildly revolting mash.

But something had been grating at the back of my mind, and I finally brought it up. "So what did Daniel say after the show?"

Kip pressed a plastic fork down hard into the cake mess before answering. "He said he always knew actors were so gay and now he has proof."

"Proof?"

"You know—dressing like a girl. Acting a girl's part. It doesn't 'prove' anything, except in Daniel-land."

"What did you say?"

"I didn't say anything. What can you say to Daniel? He always comes back with something else. I was going to try to ignore him. But then Samantha came up and said something. And it was weird. He called her a 'lesbo geek'—what else can you expect?—but then he left. I swear he was just warming up to his usual insults—until she said two magic words."

"What were they?" I had personally been looking for two magic anti-Daniel words for a long time.

"She said 'first grade.'"

—

First-Grade Photo

When I went to bed that night, I was exhausted, but too wound up to go right to sleep. Once again, I ran my favorite scenes from the last show through my head like some home movie of the play. Gradually the scenes started to morph into other plays I'd been in, and I was almost asleep when my eyes flew open and I sat right up.

I knew what Samantha meant about first grade.

I got up, turned on the light, and pulled out a box from under my bed. It was crammed with old photos. I dumped them onto the floor and started shuffling through them. After half an hour, I decided it was hopeless and went back to bed.

The next morning, I dragged myself out of bed, stepping on the slick pile, almost slipping on my butt. I looked down in annoyance and did a double take. I was almost standing on the picture I'd been looking for in the night. I picked it up and looked at it carefully. Yes, I'd remembered right. You could tell who everybody was.

The picture showed a row of kids from my first-grade class at Dover Elementary School, standing on a little stage. We had been in a classroom production of *Sleeping Beauty*. There I was on the end, dressed as the king, Sleeping Beauty's father. I was next to a kid named Jeff, who was the prince, and next to him was Samantha, as the evil thirteenth fairy. I counted eleven more girls I barely remembered, in a variety of fairy outfits.

Finding enough girls to be all thirteen fairies had

turned out to be hard. And the proof was there: in the middle of the picture, standing on tiptoe, his arms raised, was Daniel Brickster. And he was dressed as a fairy, too.

—

All in the Timing

At school, I thought about timing. I remembered telling Kip all those months ago about how important it was, about how it meant *The Sweet Tooth of Death* would win the contest. I had been wrong then, but I still believed in the principle of good timing. I intended to test that principle today.

I got to school extra early and made a trip to the computer room. I scanned the photo, cropped it, enlarged it, and printed out ten color copies. Then I carefully cut off the ends on the paper cutter.

I waited until lunchtime. I was eating with Kip and several kids from the cast—Rusty, José, Neesha, and Samantha. I handed each of them one of my copies. I had stored the original and a spare copy in my locker.

"That's it! That's the play we were in!" said Samantha excitedly, when she got her copy. "Who else are you showing these to?" she asked.

"Guess," I said.

Some people are just too predictable. It wasn't long before Daniel and his pals, Jack and Eric, walked deliberately, slowly, by our table.

"Oh, my God, it's the singing fag gang!" Daniel feigned surprise. "Good to see you've got your own table." He turned to his friends. "Don't touch it, guys—it could turn you queer."

Jack and Eric loved that one. No one at the table said anything. Kids nearby stopped talking and turned to look. I had to work hard at concentrating on my timing principle and not freak out.

Daniel went on. "Maybe you should see if the school will paint it pink for you. Wouldn't that be *special?*"

I looked up. "Hey, Daniel, we were just talking about you."

"Ooh, Daniel, he loves you!" snickered Jack.

"Why didn't *you* try out for the play?" I asked. "You used to love being in plays."

"Oh, listen to the lead queer himself. Forget it, Tutu Boy. Taking my baby sister to your stupid show was as close as I'm getting to drama queens," said Daniel, cracking himself up.

"Really?" I said. I gave an exaggerated shrug. "Funny. That's not how it looks in this picture."

"What picture? Give me that!" I was not surprised when Daniel snatched the photocopy out of my hand.

"Hey, is that you?" asked Jack and Eric together, jostling each other to get a better look.

But Daniel was quickly ripping the photo into little pieces. He leaned forward to do something like stuff them down my shirt (or somewhere worse), when

Samantha held up her copy to Jack and Eric. "You can see this one, if you want."

Daniel was lunging for it, when all the other kids held up theirs. My timing principle had taken on a life of its own.

Now Jack and Eric each had a copy to look at.

"Hey, it's not me, okay?" said Daniel. "These gays just had a little Photoshop fun. Forget it." But he was pale and his cool stance looked forced.

"It is you! Geez, what are you wearing?" Eric pointed at the picture.

In my most helpful voice, I said, "I think they might be tiny wings."

—

The Final Resting Place

Days turned into weeks, and the box of Button's ashes was still on the mantelpiece. I found a picture of me playing with him when Button was a kitten and leaned it on the wall, behind the box. Not to be outdone, Molly got one of herself when she was four, holding a full-grown Button by the armpits. Mom and Dad added pictures, and, after a while, it seemed rude to stick Button's box out in the backyard, where he'd be so far from the family action. The box stayed on the mantel.

—

What's in a Name?

"When are you going to get a new cat?" asked Kip, as we rode the bus one rainy January morning.

"Molly's been bugging our parents to do it soon," I said. "Not that there are any kittens around this time of year. She wants to name it Mr. Muffin Man Blakely."

"Sounds like a harsh thing to do to a kitten," said Kip.

"You're not kidding," I said. "Who ever heard of naming a cat for a horse?"

"What name would you pick?" Kip asked.

"Beats me. I haven't really thought about it." I shrugged.

"Liar. I bet you have a name all picked out. Come on, what is it?"

"Okay, maybe I do. Guess."

"*Guess?* Are you nuts? Okay, um, Barney."

"No way."

"Daffy Duck."

"Come on, be serious."

"I could do this all day and not guess it," said Kip. "What about Topher Junior?"

"Close. Rumpelstiltskin."

Kip laughed. "Not Detective Slade? Where's your loyalty? And like I can really hear you out at night, calling 'Here Rumpelstiltskin, here Rumpelstiltskin, come here, kitty!'"

"Well, I guess he'd have to have a nickname," I said. "Rumpy or Skinny or something. I'll figure that out when I get the cat."

The bus stopped and everyone piled out. The five-minute bell rang.

"But I know one thing already," I said, as we hurried along. "I'm going to be an actor my whole life. I'm going to be in lots of plays, even lots of musicals, and I'm going to be in one of those touring companies and visit tons of cities, and I'll be taking solo bows on Broadway. And I'll have all the cats I want, and I'll name them whatever I want, and we'll stay in great hotels with cat room service, and I'll teach them to poop in the toilet—I saw a show where a cat could do that—so I won't have to travel with a litter box, and I'm going to . . . *oomph th hph!*"

My jacket had been pulled over my head, and Kip was laughing and telling me to shut up. So I did. For now. But I was just warming up. I had a lot more to say.

You can't keep a good actor down.